COLETTE, INC. E-MAIL

TO: Jayne, Lila, Meredith
FROM: Sylvie
SUBJECT: Marcus Grey—the man I'm supposed to hate!

Marcus Grey is supposed to be the enemy, right? Well, then, how come he's all I can think about? First we shared that one fantastic dinner—which went from being strictly business to anything but! And now, everywhere I turn, there he is—at work, on the phone—asking me out for more dinners. And I don't even try to avoid him or refuse his invitations. It's as if I'm in a trance whenever I hear his voice or see him looking at me with that intense gaze, and all I can do is nod my head and say yes. What's *wrong* with me? This man is about to destroy the company we work for, and all I can do is dream about him…and what we plan to do next. <g> Now, tell me, am I just acting like a girl in lust…or more like a woman in love?

Dear Reader,

Welcome to Silhouette Desire! We're delighted to offer you again this month six passionate, powerful and provocative romances sure to please you.

Start with December's fabulous MAN OF THE MONTH, *A Cowboy's Promise*. This latest title in Anne McAllister's popular CODE OF THE WEST miniseries features a rugged Native American determined to win back the woman he left three years before. Then discover *The Secret Life of Connor Monahan* in Elizabeth Bevarly's tale of a vice cop who mistakenly surmises that a prim and proper restaurateur is operating a call-girl ring.

The sizzling miniseries 20 AMBER COURT concludes with Anne Marie Winston's *Risqué Business*, in which a loyal employee tries to prevent a powerful CEO with revenge on his mind from taking over the company she thinks of as her family. Reader favorite Maureen Child delivers the next installment of another exciting miniseries, THE FORTUNES OF TEXAS: THE LOST HEIRS. In *Did You Say Twins?!* a marine sergeant inherits twin daughters and is forced to turn for help to the woman who refused his marriage proposal ten years before.

The sexy hero of *Michael's Temptation,* the last book in Eileen Wilks's TALL, DARK & ELIGIBLE miniseries, goes to Central America to rescue a lovely lady who's been captured by guerrillas. And sparks fly when a smooth charmer and a sassy tomboy are brought together by their shared inheritance of an Australian horse farm in Brownyn Jameson's *Addicted to Nick*.

Take time out from the holiday rush and treat yourself to all si of these not-to-be-missed romances.

Enjoy,

Joan Marlow Golan

Joan Marlow Golan
Senior Editor, Silhouette Desire

Please address questions and book requests to:
Silhouette Reader Service
U.S.: 3010 Walden Ave., P.O. Box 1325, Buffalo, NY 14269
Canadian: P.O. Box 609, Fort Erie, Ont. L2A 5X3

RISQUÉ BUSINESS

ANNE MARIE WINSTON

Silhouette® Desire®

Published by Silhouette Books

America's Publisher of Contemporary Romance

Special thanks and acknowledgment are given
to Anne Marie Winston for her contribution
to the 20 AMBER COURT series.

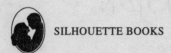 SILHOUETTE BOOKS

ISBN 0-373-76407-3

RISQUÉ BUSINESS

ANNE MARIE WINSTON

RITA Award nominee and bestselling author Anne Marie Winston loves babies she can give back when they cry, animals in all shapes and sizes and just about anything that blooms. When she's not writing, she's chauffeuring children to various activities, trying *not* to eat chocolate or reading anything she can find. She will dance at the slightest provocation and weeds her gardens when she can't see the sun for the weeds anymore. You can learn more about Anne Marie's novels by visiting her Web site at www.annemariewinston.com.

For my Morgan May
I love you bunches, even if you can beat me at mancala.

One

Sylvie Bennett closed the door of 4A and headed down the stairs of her apartment building at 20 Amber Court. As she reached the head of the sweeping marble staircase that led to the foyer, her brisk pace slowed. Through the leaded glass panes surrounding the heavy front door, she could see fat white snowflakes falling over Youngsville, Indiana, her hometown.

Great, she thought in disgust. A lake-effect snowstorm was the last thing she needed today. Normally she enjoyed walking to work rather than taking the bus. But this morning, she wanted to look particularly crisp and professional. Chapped cheeks and wild, wind-whipped hair didn't fit that profile one little bit.

Her normally buoyant spirits sank even lower as she thought about what she intended to do today. She was entirely likely to be trudging the long blocks home without a job tonight.

"Sylvie! Good morning!"

Her morose mood vanished at the sight of her landlady, Rose Carson. A pretty flannel robe covered Rose's generous curves and her salt-and-pepper curls were tousled as if she hadn't bothered to brush her hair yet. She looked warm and approachable and...totally huggable, thought Sylvie whimsically. If she'd ever dreamed of having a mother, which she hadn't allowed herself to do in a very long time, Rose would fit the bill. She treasured their friendship. "Hi. How are you this morning?" She descended the steps and crossed the foyer to Rose's door, where the older woman stood with her newspaper in hand.

"I am marvelous," Rose said brightly. "I have a feeling something wonderful is going to happen today!"

Sylvie smiled wryly, recalling her thoughts from a moment earlier. "That would be nice." She laid her coat over the banister and began to wrap her woolen scarf snugly about her neck.

"That's a lovely suit, dear." Rose reached out her hand and gently smoothed the fabric of one lapel. "But, if you'll forgive me, I think you need something striking to set it off."

"Probably," Sylvie agreed. "But what good jewelry I own would fit on the head of a pin."

Rose's eyes twinkled. "Shame on you, young lady! You work for one of the most prestigious jewelry houses in the country and you don't have any of your own?" Her eyes lit up and she raised a hand, indicating that Sylvie should wait a minute. "I have just the thing."

"Rose, you don't have to—" But her landlady dashed back into her apartment before Sylvie could complete the sentence. She was back again within the minute.

"Here we go." Rose held up a stunning brooch fashioned of precious metals. Several pieces of clear golden amber glittered amid a cluster of other gems. Although it wasn't quite heart-shaped, Sylvie's first thought was that Rose was giving Sylvie her heart to wear.

"I couldn't possibly—oh, it's beautiful." Sylvie inspected the piece in the hall mirror. "This is spectacular. Where did you find it? Who made it?"

"A designer I knew a long time ago." Rose dismissed the topic, reaching forward to position the brooch against Sylvie's lapel. "This is exactly what you need today."

"Oh, I couldn't. It's too valuable—"

"And it does nothing but gather dust in my jewelry case," Rose interjected. Her nimble fingers fastened the pin into place. "There. Look how stunning that is." She took Sylvie's shoulders and turned her to the mirror hanging above the small marble-topped table beside the umbrella stand in the foyer.

"It *is* perfect, isn't it?" Sylvie touched the brooch with a gentle finger. She needed all the self-confidence she could get today. Perhaps she would borrow this from Rose, just this once. "All right." She turned with a smile, leaning forward to press a kiss to Rose's smooth cheek. "You win. I'll wear it."

"Perfect!" Rose clapped her hands together like an excited child. "You'd better get going, dear. I know you like to get into the office early and it will be a little slippery today, judging from the view out my window."

Sylvie nodded as she finished winding her scarf around her mouth and neck and donned her long winter duster, tugging its hood well up over her head. "Wish me luck. I have an important meeting today." Well, that wasn't a lie. The fact that she hadn't been invited to the meeting was beside the point.

"Luck." Rose held up crossed fingers on both hands. "With that brooch on, I can practically guarantee it."

Sylvie wrestled open the front door, holding it to keep the wind from slamming it shut. Rose's last comment barely registered. "Thanks again, Rose. I'll see you tonight."

"Stop, Mr. Grey! What you're proposing may be legal, but it's immoral."

Two hours after arriving at work, Sylvie barged into the conference room and strode purposefully toward the long table around which were seated the board members of Colette, Inc., the jewelry company for which she had worked for the past five years. The company at which she'd finally, for the first time in her life, felt as if she fit in. Colette and its employees were her *family* and nobody was going to mess with Sylvie's family.

A ripple of surprise worked its way around the room in response to her intrusion, but Sylvie barely noticed. All her attention was focused on the man slowly rising to his feet at the head of the table.

Her stomach balled into a tight fist of nerves at her own audacity. But someone had to do it!

She kept her gaze squarely focused on Marcus Grey, the unethical cretin who was trying to ruin Colette. As she got closer and her eyes locked with his, another sensation flitted into her stomach. Lord, but the man didn't look like the few pictures she'd seen in the newspapers. And he *really* didn't look a thing like the picture of an ogre which her imagination had steadily embellished.

No, he couldn't look less like an ogre if he'd been a prince. She felt a strong tug of purely physical attraction. He had a square jaw with a chin that thrust aggressively forward, strong white teeth and lean, clean-shaven cheeks. His skin was tan and blended perfectly with his gleaming tawny hair. Too perfectly. The color made his green eyes gleam with the deep rich color of an emerald. Below the aquiline blade of his strong nose was a thin-lipped, wide mouth—a mouth that was curving up at the moment with entirely inappropriate amusement.

She felt her cheeks flush with heat as she returned his stare. *Anger,* she told herself. So what if the man was good-looking. He was still an ogre in her book.

He merely watched her for the longest time, never breaking the eye contact. Well, she wouldn't, either. Businesspeople were like dogs—the one who outstared the other had the upper hand, and she'd go blind before she'd give him an inch. But as his glowing eyes continued to devour her, the sensation was so unnerving that she finally had to look away. She guessed it was a good thing she wasn't a dog, because Marcus Grey was never going to be the leader of her pack.

"Since I have yet to propose anything, I fail to see the immorality in attending a meeting of the board of directors. I *am* the majority stockholder." Grey's voice was cool and even. Despite the smile, which to her critical eye looked distinctly smug, his teeth snapped together over every word in a manner that suggested he'd like to snap them on *her.*

"I've heard all about your schemes," Sylvie said, coming to a halt in front of him. She shook a finger at him as she spoke. "We all have, here at Colette. We—" she paused for emphasis, "are a family, Mr. Grey, and we will not permit you to destroy us."

Thick eyebrows rose. Very deliberately, he allowed his gaze to trail down her body, lingering in the vicinity of her bosom before moving slowly to her toes. Hot temper rose; she had to struggle against the urge to kick him in a place that would ensure he had no desire to look at another woman like that for quite a while. At the same time, it felt as if he'd left a trail of fire everywhere his gaze had touched. It was an effort to keep her breathing level as her heart began to thud in her breast. *You're supposed to be offended by that!* she told her traitorous body.

When his eyes finally met hers again, he was smiling even more widely. "You have me at a disadvantage, Ms…?"

"Bennett," she snapped, annoyed with herself for getting giddy just because he was one totally, amazingly mouthwatering hunk of man. "Assistant Director of Marketing."

"Ms. Bennett," he repeated. "And what vile schemes am I supposed to have concocted to destroy this company?"

Her lip curled. "Since you were served with an injunction to prevent you from liquidating Colette's holdings, I don't imagine you need a rundown of your intentions."

"The lawsuit was dismissed, if you'll recall," he said mildly, "for lack of evidence." He cocked his head and studied her for a long moment while she searched for a suitable reply. Then, to her surprise, he stepped forward and took her elbow. "Come with me, Ms. Bennett."

"I beg your pardon?" She told herself she was allowing him to escort her from the room, though the fingers that enclosed her arm felt suspiciously like a handcuff and just about as unyielding. If she'd dug in her heels, of course, he wouldn't have been able to budge her.

As he excused himself from the meeting and moved with her toward the door, an unexpected sight caught her attention. Rose stood quietly by the buffet spread, her hands folded at the waist of her sturdy navy blue suit...*Rose?*

Sylvie nearly stumbled as Marcus Grey towed her along in his wake. As Sylvie passed her, the older woman gave her a discreet thumbs-up and winked. What the heck was Rose doing at a Colette board meeting?

Sylvie's stomach clenched again as one of the waiters scurried past in his white shirt and navy pants. Navy suit...Rose was wearing a uniform! Dear Lord, if her circumstances were so dire that she had to take a second job to make ends meet, why on earth hadn't she raised the rents? Sylvie fought guilt as she recalled the delight she'd felt when she'd been offered the beautiful apartment and realized its modest rental was easily within her limited means. She'd have to talk to the other tenants about this as soon as possible. Rose was fifty-six years old, for Heaven's sake. While she certainly wasn't in her dotage, working as a glorified waitress had to be hard on her. Sylvie herself had worked as a waitress to help pay her college expenses. It was darn hard work!

They reached the heavy wood-paneled door of the conference room and Grey held it open for her, then stepped into the hallway after her.

She tore her elbow from his grasp the moment he stopped and immediately turned to face him, all her attention zeroing in on her goal once again. "You won't get rid of me so easily," she warned. "You can't simply dismantle Colette while all of us who love it stand idly by."

Gone was the smile. And in its place was an implacable determination that almost shook her resolve. "I'm the majority stockholder now. I can do anything I want with this company and there's not a thing any of you can do to prevent it."

"We'll file another injunction." She realized she was fiddling with the beautifully wrought amber brooch Rose had insisted on loaning her before she'd left the apartment building earlier that morning and she forced herself to still her hands.

"A temporary snag." He dismissed the threat of another lawsuit as if it were no more than a mildly pesky fly at a picnic.

That *did* shake her, but she'd be darned if she'd let him see it. She switched tactics. "What can I offer you, Mr. Grey, to put aside your plans?"

The eyebrows rose again. His eyes gleamed like those of a big cat scenting prey. "Is that a personal or professional offer, Ms. Bennett?"

She felt hot color sweep up into her cheeks as an entirely unprofessional image of herself locked in his arms popped into her head. "Purely professional, I assure you. Everyone at Colette shares the same commitment to this company that I do."

He regarded her silently for a moment. "What's your first name?"

"I—what?"

The corners of his mouth lifted the slightest bit. "What's your first name, Ms. Bennett?"

"Sylvie." Nonplussed, she spread her hands. "Why?"

"I wanted to know what name goes with such a fetching package."

She blushed again, even more annoyed because of the surge of pleasure she'd felt at the compliment. "Sexual harassment is an ugly charge, Mr. Grey. Watch it."

"Call me Marcus." He ignored her flash of temper. "Sylvie, could we make a deal?"

She regarded him with suspicion. "Such as?"

"Dinner. You and me. Tonight. In exchange for which

I promise not to take any actions in that board meeting today that would adversely affect Colette, Inc.''

Now her eyebrows rose. "Why on earth would you want to have dinner with me?"

"Because you're an attractive woman and I like your style." His gaze sharpened. "And because you've intrigued me. What would make an employee feel so strongly about a company in which she doesn't have anything invested? There are probably other, better jobs out there for a sharp, ambitious woman like you."

"How do you know I'm ambitious?" she shot back. "I might be perfectly content with my position here."

He snorted. "And pigs fly. Like recognizes like, Sylvie." Then his amusement fled. "So what's your answer?"

"What happens if I refuse your dinner command?"

He smiled, all teeth and razor-edged intellect. "I thought you wanted the best for Colette, Inc.?"

Checkmate. The rat. She considered. What could be the harm? She could at least buy Colette a little more time for legal maneuvering, even if she couldn't convince him not to close down the company. And it wasn't as if he were completely loathsome. If only he weren't the man who...well, he was. And that was that. She'd enjoy matching wits with him.

"I suppose," she said slowly, "that I'm forced to accept. Do I have your word you won't take any action today?"

He raised one hand, a sardonic smile on his face. "Word of honor."

"Huh." She turned to leave. "As if that's worth anything. An honorable person wouldn't consider putting more than one hundred people out of work."

"Who said anything about putting people out of work?"

"Isn't that what you're planning to do?" She looked back at him and threw out a direct challenge.

"I'm planning on making a profitable business deal," he said with the first hint of testiness she'd heard.

"Regardless of who gets hurt." Her voice was scornful as she started back to her office.

"Ms. Bennett." His tone was quiet, yet it never occurred to her to ignore him.

Slowly she swung back to meet his gaze.

"I know far more about people getting hurt by corporate wheeling and dealing than you could imagine. I always consider the employees in my equations."

And just what had happened to him? she wondered later. She closed the door of her office after receiving a lackluster dressing down for her impetuous behavior from her boss, who apparently couldn't bring himself to be really annoyed by her actions. Unless she was mistaken, Marcus Grey's bitter words had been clear. Apparently he felt he'd been wronged by some unfortunate business deals...could they have involved Colette? That might explain the way he was going after the company.

Acting on impulse, she got online and began a search. If she had to go out to dinner with him tonight, she intended to know everything there was to know about Marcus Grey. Including any event in his life that would have precipitated his last cryptic words.

As he climbed into his gleaming black Mercedes coupe that evening, Marcus thought of the way Sylvie Bennett had stalked down the hall after they'd parted, her short, pleated autumn-brown skirt swishing back and forth around shapely legs.

He'd always wondered how men could allow themselves to be ruled by their glands. In the numerous associations with women he'd had over the years, he'd never been the one to lose control, never been so swept up by emotion that he lost his reason. Despite the fact that he thoroughly enjoyed passionate encounters with the fairer sex, a part of his brain had always been fully functional.

Until today. Did she have any idea how gorgeous she was, with her dark gypsy eyes and full, eminently kissable lips? He'd had trouble concentrating on what she was saying because he'd been too busy watching the way her delectable lips formed every syllable, the way her breasts had so very nicely filled out the jacket of her suit, the way her silky hair had swung around her animated face as she shook her head.

If anyone else had barged into that conference room and started haranguing him, he'd have had their head on his dinner platter. But when Sylvie had started across the room, he'd been unable to do much more than stare. He'd fallen into her dark eyes without even raising a hand for rescue. Her silky suit molded her figure in a way he doubted she realized, and he'd been able to hear the gentle swish of her silk stockings as her legs had brushed when she walked across the floor. The sound was such a turn-on that the small part of him still able to think at all had been momentarily speechless at the intense sensations rushing through him.

Finally, she'd looked away from him and it was as if a spell had been broken. And as her words sank in, he had stopped thinking about how fast he could get her into the sack and started listening to the not-so-veiled hostility in her husky voice.

What in hell were people saying about him? This gossip must have been the catalyst for that ridiculous and ultimately unsuccessful lawsuit the board of Colette had lodged against him.

True, he *did* plan to absorb Colette and shut down the jewelry manufacturer completely, but it wasn't as if he were going to kick all its employees out on the street. Oh, there would be a certain amount of housecleaning; he didn't tolerate inefficiency or dead weight. But for the most part, the employees of Colette, Inc. would become employees of Grey Enterprises. And he'd told the board members that when he'd returned to the meeting after talking with Sylvie Bennett. After all, if they didn't have to worry about losing their jobs, why would they care where they worked?

The board meeting. He could still recall the bewilderment and relief on the faces of the board members when he hadn't made any motions to start the process that would annihilate Colette. They obviously didn't understand why he had delayed.

He didn't completely understand it himself.

But the swell of vindication, of at-long-last pleasure he'd felt for so long was subdued for the first time since he'd grown old enough, and rich enough, to realize he had the means to avenge his father's humiliation and eventual self-destruction at the hands of Colette, Inc. Sylvie Bennett had succeeded in humanizing the company, a circumstance he'd never considered. Never wanted to consider.

It was just a company.

And, he thought, Sylvie Bennett was just a woman, albeit a woman like no other he'd ever met. He'd do well to remember that.

He was used to women fawning over him. As an eligible bachelor with a fortune at his disposal, he supposed he'd be considered a catch even if he looked like a toad. Which, judging from the ease with which he had charmed women all his life, he was pretty sure was not the case.

Sylvie Bennett hadn't fawned. And she hadn't appeared to be particularly charmed, either, though he knew with some deep, basic instinct that she'd been as aware of him as he'd been of her. What she'd appeared to be was furious. He'd found himself ridiculously drawn to the sparkling ire in her big dark eyes. He'd had to remind himself that he couldn't simply grab her and plunder all her delightful treasures until the fire he sensed inside her roared free and consumed them both. He couldn't kiss the frown from her face, couldn't drag her lush curves against him and fill himself with her, couldn't take her into the nearest private room and feast on her silky skin.

But, oh, how he'd wanted to. And he still did. She might think she was going to talk him into some pansy-ass emotional generosity regarding her precious company tonight, but he had other plans. And those plans included getting to know everything there was to know about Ms. Sylvie Bennett as soon as he could talk his way around that protective streak she felt for Colette. And eventually—his blood quickened as he remembered the way her eyes had flashed—it was entirely likely that he was going to have to get the delectable Ms. Bennett into his bed.

He knew she was unmarried, because the instant that damned meeting had ended, he'd checked out her personnel file. Single, twenty-seven years old, had worked for the company since her graduation from college. Repeatedly receiving glowing performance reviews, she was clearly a rising star on Colette's corporate ladder. He knew her height, five-foot-three, and her weight, one hundred twenty-one handsomely curvaceous pounds. The one thing he hadn't found was any information about her family. She'd listed no next-of-kin, had merely noted that in the event of an emergency her landlady should be advised. Practical. Did that mean she had no family?

He pulled the Mercedes sports car into a parking place in front of the soaring mansion-turned-apartments where he'd noted Sylvie lived, admiring the grace with which the old building had aged. He'd had his secretary call and tell her to be ready to go to dinner at seven-thirty. He figured they'd follow that up with drinks at either his place or hers...and he'd take it from there.

Oh, indeed he would.

She opened the door moments after his first knock.

"Good evening, Mr. Grey. Would you like to come in?" Her dark gaze was unsmiling.

"Thank you." He stepped past her, turning as she shut the door behind him. "For you." He held out the florist's box he'd brought with him from the car.

Sylvie took it from him with a look so suspicious that he nearly laughed aloud. "It's not a package bomb." Hmm, better revise his estimated timetable for making love to her. It might take longer than he'd supposed to get as close to her as he wanted to get.

Her eyebrows relaxed at his words. Hesitantly, she said, "Thank you."

Then, as she uncovered the fragile white orchids he'd nursed through the cold Indiana air, she exclaimed, "Oh!" and gave him a far more sincere, "Thank you." She lifted the satiny petals and brushed them against her cheek and he was struck by the contrast between the pale blossom and the soft pink of her skin. "These are lovely." Her gaze warmed and she smiled at him.

Then again, there might be hope for the evening after all.

She had deep dimples in both cheeks, making her appear both mischievous and seductive at the same time. He wanted to touch the skin of her cheek to see if it really was as soft as it looked, to press his lips to one of the little puckers that her dimples made in her otherwise flawless complexion. Her lips were outlined in hot, glossy red and as thoughts of what that beautifully bowed red mouth could do to him paraded through his head, he realized it was going to be a long dinner. Sitting and watching her delicately eat morsel after morsel was going to be more of an exercise in self-control than he'd known in some time.

She gestured to the high-ceiling living room decorated in stark white with striking accents of sapphire, hot pink and emerald, its modern look accented by glass-and-chrome tables. "Would you like to sit down?"

"No, thank you," he replied. "We have dinner reservations at eight." He'd have bet his last dollar that her décor would be striking and distinctive, much like Sylvie herself.

She matched her living room's bold ambience tonight. She was in red, hot red that exactly matched her lipstick. A color, he suspected, that she donned when declaring war. The dress was simple, deceptively so. A figure-hugging sheath with long sleeves, it had a modest neckline that revealed no hint of the delectable flesh beneath. It needed none, though. The red silk faithfully followed every curve. And when she excused herself and turned toward the kitchen to get a container for the flowers he'd bought, he saw that the back of the dress came over her shoulders and plunged to her waist, leaving a large vee of flawless ivory flesh revealed.

His interest level shot up yet another notch. If she'd wanted to make a statement, she'd succeeded, he thought wryly. Perhaps it had been a shrewdly calculated move as well—he was definitely going to have trouble keeping his mind on business tonight and he suspected she knew it.

Still, the essential untamed male in him couldn't help speculating. How could a woman wear a bra beneath a dress like that? The answer, in his mind, was clear. She couldn't.

Now how the heck was he supposed to carry on a conversation while half his brain was occupied with wondering how easy it would be to slide his hand beneath the edges of that daring little dress? How long it would take for him to inch his way around to the soft feminine treasures he sought? How long before he could talk her out of it entirely?

He sighed. He was thinking like a jerk. And the worst part was, he couldn't remember the last time a woman had enticed him enough that his brain circuits got scrambled like this. He'd been working too hard.

She returned a moment later with a hot pink glazed vase in a modern Oriental motif containing his orchids, giving him another sweet smile. Then she showed him her back again when she set them down in the middle of the oval glass table in her dining area.

"All right." She turned and lifted a long white wool coat from the back of a chair. "I'm ready."

He took the coat from her. As he held it for her to slide into, he couldn't resist letting his hands linger on her shoulders for a moment. A heady floral scent drifted up to tease his nostrils and he inhaled deeply. It was perfect for her—essentially feminine but with secretive accents beneath the beauty.

As he escorted her down the wide marble staircase, the door to apartment 1A opened. An attractive older woman stepped out, carrying a casserole dish. With a small sense of shock, he recognized the woman who'd attended the stockholders meeting this afternoon, the other Colette stockholder.

"Hello, Rose," said Sylvie.

"Hello, dear. Going out for the evening?"

Sylvie nodded. He could practically sense the reluctance radiating from her at the idea of introducing him to her neighbor. "Rose, this is Marcus Grey. Marcus, my landlady and dear friend, Rose Carson."

He nodded and opened his mouth to respond but as he met the woman's eyes, she gave a single, discreet shake of her head. His eyebrows rose. Interesting. For whatever reason, she obviously didn't want Sylvie to know her connection to the company. Instead of asking the question he'd intended, he merely said, "Good evening, Mrs. Carson."

"Mr. Grey." She smiled at him, her eyes telegraphing her relief, then turned back to Sylvie. "Ella in 2D has a cold so I thought I'd take her some of my chicken-noodle soup."

Sylvie beamed at the woman. "I'm sure she'd be very grateful, Rose. That always works wonders for me. Oh! And I nearly forgot—I still have your brooch. I'll run and get it."

"No rush, dear," said Rose comfortably. "You can bring it down another time. Go out and have a lovely evening."

"Are you talking about the brooch you were wearing today?" Marcus thought for a moment. "It was striking, as I recall. Amber. A truly beautiful piece."

To his surprise, Rose Carson blushed. "It's just an old thing I treasure. It isn't extremely valuable."

"If you treasure it, then it has value," he said firmly, earning a second smile from the older woman.

Sylvie shot him a warm, approving glance. Then she turned back to Rose. "All right. I'll bring it by tomorrow. There's something I want to discuss with you, anyway."

A few moments later, as he escorted her down the wide steps, she said, "That was a nice thing to say to Rose."

He shrugged. "I meant it." They moved on to his car and he held the door for her. As she slid in, the white coat parted, baring a long length of slender thigh where her red dress had ridden up. He reached down and tucked the trailing edge of the coat into the car before she could get to it, and his pulse skyrocketed as he caught another whiff of her scent. Fate had indeed been good to him today.

He drove north of the city proper to the Youngsville Country Club, a private establishment with an extensive golf course that abutted the lovely grounds of Ingalls Park to the east and fronted the lake as well. Sylvie was quiet on the drive, a condition he suspected wasn't her usual mode of operation. Her hands were clasped together in her lap but her right thumb rubbed ceaselessly back and forth over the flesh of the other.

"I looked at your personnel file," he said abruptly. He thought he'd rather have her prickly and argumentative than wary and nervous like this.

She turned her head then, finally looking fully at him. "I beg your pardon?"

"I needed to find out where you lived." Which wasn't exactly true; his secretary could have done that.

"I thought that's what administrative assistants were for," she said.

He grinned. Had she read his mind? "Not always," he said mildly. "So. Tell me why you chose to work at Colette. I saw that you've been there for five years. Was it your first job out of college?"

She nodded. "Yes. I majored in marketing and management. When I heard that Colette might be hiring, I was thrilled. I've always loved beautiful jewelry and gems." She smiled. "Not that they're in my budget."

"And where did you start?" He already knew—it was in her file—but he wanted to make her feel more comfortable. In his experience, little made people relax faster than talking about themselves.

"I'm sure you already know." Again, he had the uncomfortable sensation that she knew exactly what he was thinking.

"Indulge me. I'd like to hear it from your point of view."

"Okay." She shrugged. "I sent Colette a resume before graduation but I didn't really have much hope. I'd heard it was terribly difficult to get a foot through the door and that people rarely left. When I got a call to interview, I was shocked. But I figured I'd make the most of it—and I did. I was hired as an assistant in the sales department, moved up to sales, over into marketing and then up again. I love what I do."

He believed it. And he suspected she was very good at working out effective marketing strategies and communicating with clients. "You could still do that with another company."

"I don't want to work for another company. I love Colette. The people I work with have become dear friends. Their spouses are my friends. I'm a godmother to my first supervisor's grandson. You can't just throw them all away." She was really getting wound up now and the smooth bell of her hair swung wide as she turned to face him. "Colette is more than just dollars, more than just points on the stock market. Why do you want to destroy it?"

It stung that she'd never once asked him to explain his position on the Colette takeover, that before she'd ever met him she was willing to believe he was a ruthless, heartless executive who sent heads rolling right and left.

"I never said I want to destroy it." He reiterated his earlier stance. If she wasn't going to give him the benefit of the doubt, he wasn't going to give her any more information than the rumor mill already had. "You and your *family* have stirred up all manner of stories that might not even be true."

"Or they might be," she tossed back. "I notice you haven't really answered my question. Won't you at least think about the people who depend on Colette for their livelihood?"

"All right." He parked the car and came around to her door to escort her into the country club.

"All right?" She stopped in her tracks like a recalcitrant mule and glared at him. "What does that mean? All right, you'll consider my point of view or all right, you've had enough of it? You can take me home right now, Mr. Grey."

Two

―――

"**W**hoa," Marcus said. "I don't want to fight with you, Sylvie."

"Well, what do you want to do then?"

He saw she regretted the words the moment they hit the air. He grinned wickedly. "First? Or afterward?"

She wasn't stupid enough to ask, "After what?" Instead, she gave him a rueful smile. "I asked for that, didn't I?"

He said, "You did, indeed." Then he put a hand beneath her elbow and started walking toward the clubhouse again. "Let's suspend all talk of our mutual point of disagreement for the rest of the evening. I don't often get the chance to wine and dine a woman as beautiful as you and I'd like to savor the moment."

She hesitated and he thought she was going to refuse to drop the subject. Then she shook her head as she walked before him through the door. "You're a smooth talker, Mr. Grey. I'll have to be on my toes."

He snorted. "I don't think you need to worry. Unless," he added, "you keep calling me Mr. Grey. My name is Marcus."

She smiled. "Marcus." The way her lips looked as she formed his name was quite possibly the most erotic sight he'd ever seen, and he fought the surge of heat that flooded his body.

He checked her coat and the maître d' led them to the table he'd reserved that looked out over Lake Michigan. A stiff wind whipped up frothy whitecaps that scudded across the steely surface of the water and they both looked out over the lake with pleasure. "Even in the winter it's beautiful," she said softly.

They shared a dry white wine and Sylvie smiled at him across the dancing candle flame. "You didn't mention that your father owned a gem and jewelry design company once upon a time. Van Arl, I believe it was called."

He froze, wineglass halfway to his mouth as her smile turned smug. Slowly, he forced himself to take a casual sip and set it down again. "Van Arl's been out of business for a long time. It's ancient history."

Her eyebrows rose. "A mere quarter-century is hardly ancient."

He shrugged. "If you say so. Where did you hear about Van Arl?"

"You aren't the only one who came prepared. I did a little background checking of my own this afternoon, without benefit of a handy-dandy personnel file."

"Great. I had to pick Sherlock Holmes for a date." He tried a smile, hoping it looked more natural than it felt, and forced himself to act nonchalant but inside his mind was rolling and pitching like a steamer on Lake Michigan in a storm. "What do you want to know about Van Arl? I was a child when it was in operation. I have very little memory of it."

"It was a real up-and-coming business for a while. Could have been competitive with Colette, couldn't it?"

"*Was* competitive with Colette in the sixties and seventies. It also supplied Colette with some fine quality gemstones at one time." He congratulated himself on the evenness of his tone. "Until Colette lured away my father's top design team, which you already know if you read anything about it."

She nodded. When his eyes met hers, the deep well of sympathy—or pity, he wasn't sure which was worse—in the chocolate depths stirred a fury he hadn't given in to in years. He didn't want her pity, damn it! "This isn't a revenge thing, if that's what you're thinking," he said, striving for cool insouciance. "But wouldn't that make for a great story?"

"It would." She took a sip of her wine and leaned forward. "Especially since Van Arl couldn't compete without those designers and the lack of notable work started affecting company profits."

He shrugged again. "Can you blame them? Colette apparently offered those people more money and better benefits than they had at Van Arl. It was merely a good career move, I'm sure. Just as my decision to take over Colette is good business."

A gleam of understanding lit her eyes. "So that's how you're rationalizing this? As good business?" She put a hand atop his on the table and he realized he was clenching his fists. "Marcus, the people that work at Colette now aren't responsible for what happened to your father's business. Carl Colette was the man who led the company way back then and he's been dead a long time. He had one daughter whom I've heard took off for parts unknown years and years ago and hasn't been heard from since. There hasn't been a Colette involved in Colette, Incorporated since Carl's widow died over a decade ago.''

"This has nothing to do with who works at Colette," he insisted. "I grew up with an interest in gems and jewelry, thanks to my father's company, and I want to continue to expand that interest. The name of the company I purchase means nothing. It's simply business. I looked for the best possible deal out there. Colette looked less stable and more attainable than any other.''

Striving to sidetrack her, he turned his hand over and captured her fingers with his, stroking his thumb lightly back and forth over the tender skin. But she wasn't deterred. Pulling her hand free, she hastily placed it in her lap.

"So you intend to keep Colette intact even if you change the name?''

"I didn't say that," he hedged. "But as I told you, I always make sure valuable employees are taken care of when I acquire a business.''

Sylvie sat back. "If you say so." Clearly she was unconvinced but he refused to be drawn in by her baiting.

"I say so," he said. Then turning his head, he summoned the waiter. Over the entrée, he managed to steer the conversation through less volatile channels. He learned that she was an aficionado of theater, particularly musical theater, and that she owned the soundtrack to every play Andrew Lloyd Weber ever staged. They discovered they had seen some of the same shows last summer at a local summer theatre that brought in high-quality talent and on whose board he sat.

"How did you get interested in theater?" he asked. "Did you have family involved in performing arts?"

"I just enjoy a good show." She had been smiling at him but at the words, she looked away, out over the lake. "I never even saw a play until I was in high school," she said. "I was—am—an orphan."

"I'm sorry. I didn't mean to bring up painful memories." He reached across the table and covered one of her hands as she had done to him earlier.

"It's all right." She took a breath and he could see the effort it took her to smile.

"Weren't you adopted?"

Sylvie shook her head. She turned her striking gypsy eyes on him again and gave him a small, rueful smile. "I was a sickly baby and a bratty little kid. If I were a prospective parent, I'd have run the other way when I saw a kid like me, too." Her words were glib and flippant, so much so that he realized there was pain lurking below.

"Sounds like a rotten way to grow up."

She shrugged, her smile set. "It was all right. I rarely think about it anymore since my life got straightened out."

He was intrigued by the odd phrasing. "Since your life got straightened out? You make it sound as if you're an ex-con."

She chuckled, and some of the tension left the set of her shoulders. "No. But I probably was well on my way to prison. I was a wild child."

"How wild? Picking-fights-wild or are we talking tying people to their bedposts and stealing the silver?"

This time, her laugh was genuine. "Neither. I had a foolproof method for dealing with foster homes I didn't like. I just kept running away until they got sick of trying to contain me. After the fourth or fifth home, they sent me to a school for juveniles on the brink of delinquency. It was run like a military institution and I hated it at first, but the discipline was exactly what I needed.'' She spread her arms wide and shot him a mischievous grin.

''I became the model citizen you see today.''

He snorted. ''I suspect you're still a rabble-rouser at heart.'' But as the waiter came to clear their table, he couldn't help wondering how Sylvie had become the successful, ebullient person she was. Her childhood sounded like a genuine nightmare. To whom had she turned for love and security? While his own childhood had been far from perfect, he'd always known he was loved by both of his parents. Even when things went wrong between them after his father's business failed, Marcus had never doubted that he'd been loved. For the first time, it occurred to him that there were worse things than having your parents split up, even if it was hard to see that as a child.

As they were sharing coffee, the trio of musicians that had been providing dinner music switched gears and began to play sedate ballroom dance tunes. Around them, several couples rose and headed for the dance floor.

''Would you like to dance?'' He hadn't brought her here with the conscious intent of getting her into his arms, but since the opportunity presented itself, he wasn't going to miss it.

''I'd love to.'' She rose and let him lead her onto the dance floor, where he took her in a very proper dance position and began to whirl her around to the strains of a waltz. She was a good dancer, light on her feet and quick to follow his lead, and he pressed her into more and more intricate steps, delighted when she didn't miss a beat.

His hand was splayed across the soft, bare skin of her back as he guided her through the patterns. Beneath his fingertips, she felt like warm silk. He was very conscious that she wasn't wearing a bra and he found he had to work to keep his gaze from straying to her breasts. As the music swelled, he moved her in a series of quick, spinning turns that forced her body against his. Their legs tangled and his breath caught in his chest at the feel of her gentle curves against him. Each time their eyes met, he saw in her gaze the same helpless sexual fascination with which he was wrestling.

Abruptly, he spun her out and took her across the floor once more. He'd wanted women before, had held their sweet scented bodies, had kissed their eager lips, but if he'd ever wanted a woman the way he wanted this woman, he couldn't recall it. The strong tug of attraction between them made him nervous. But he wasn't going to ignore it.

They were both laughing after a particularly energetic swing when an older woman on her way to the door stopped and said, "You two dance beautifully together. You must get a lot of practice."

Sylvie turned and smiled at the woman, patting Marcus on the arm. "We dance frequently."

As the woman moved on, Marcus couldn't contain his chuckle. "Liar."

"I wasn't lying." Sylvie lifted her nose in the air. "I do dance frequently. And so do you or you couldn't be that good. She just assumed we dance *together*."

He laughed harder. "You're a slippery one. Remind me never to take anything you say at face value."

Then the music slowed and his laughter died away as he stared down into her wide eyes. He drew her closer, folding his fingers around hers and drawing her hand against his chest. Her hand was small and warm in his and he inhaled the clean fragrance of her curly, black hair. Their bodies brushed lightly as they moved and her face was so close he could rest his lips against her temple if he turned his head. It was a tempting idea, but he restrained himself.

They swayed in silence for a while. His hand slowly stroked the silken skin of her back and despite the strong sexual pull that rose between them, he could feel himself relaxing, muscle by muscle, as an overwhelming feeling of *rightness* soothed his mind. He wanted her, but that could wait. Right now, it felt wonderful to simply hold her. "This is nice," he murmured.

"Um-hmm. Very nice." She curled her fingers around his shoulder and sighed.

"Sylvie...I'm enjoying being with you." And he was, on far more than a physical level. She was bright and witty and articulate and she wasn't afraid to argue with him. She was the most appealing woman he'd met in, well, forever. She was unique.

"I'm enjoying it, too," she said softly. "Too much."

"How can you enjoy something too much?" The idea made him smile.

She leaned back slightly in his embrace and looked up at him. "You know what I mean. We're on opposite sides of what looks like it could become a very nasty little war."

"That's business. This is personal." He drew her even closer, until their thighs met and he could feel her full breasts against his chest. She didn't stiffen, didn't pull away, but came against him with a quiet sigh. He soaked in the quiet, intimate pleasure of dancing so closely with her, enjoying the tug of arousal her nearness produced in his loins. "Very personal."

"I'm not sure we can separate the two." But she snuggled closer, turning her head into his neck.

"I am. Why don't we agree to disagree on that topic?" he suggested, nuzzling his nose into her hair. "And leave it at that."

"I…a—all right." She sounded as if she were having trouble connecting her thoughts, a feeling with which he could identify. A fierce satisfaction swept through him. He'd been afraid he was the only one feeling as if he were sinking for the third time.

He could feel the warmth of her breath and imagine that her lips would touch him at any moment. Unable to resist, he slipped his arms fully around her, aligning her sweet curves with his aching body, and the sensation was so exquisite he nearly groaned aloud when she raised her arms and encircled his neck.

"Look up," he commanded her.

But she shook her head. "No."

"Why not?"

A bubble of husky laughter followed his question. "Because if I do, you'll kiss me. And I don't think I'm ready to deal with kisses from you."

He grinned above her head. Her honesty was unexpected. He liked it. "I *know* I'm not ready to deal with kissing you," he said, "but I want to anyway."

"People don't always get what they want," she said with a hint of asperity. "Or didn't your privileged upbringing ever teach you that truth?"

Her words struck a nerve. He stopped dancing and waited until she finally glanced up at him. "I did grow up with money," he said quietly, "and I can't deny it made my life comfortable in many ways. But don't ever assume money brings you everything you want."

Sylvie looked stricken, her eyes dark with remorse.

"Marcus, I—I'm sorry. That was an unforgivably rude thing to say."

"Apology accepted." He pressed his lips to her forehead. "Do you want to kiss me to make up for it?"

Her pretty face dissolved into a smile that made her dimples flash. "You're certainly persistent."

He nodded gravely. "It's one of my finer qualities."

"No kissing," she said. "Especially not in public."

"Ah, she gives me hope. How about in private?"

Her only response was a mock-glare and he laughed as he took her hand and led her from the dance floor. "Are you ready to leave?"

"Yes." She glanced at her watch. "But not because I intend to get hot and heavy with you, mister. I have to work tomorrow."

Chuckling, he retrieved her coat and helped her into it.

When they arrived at Amber Court, he escorted her from the car up to her apartment. As they mounted the stairs, he could see her withdrawing from him, pulling back and erecting the defenses he thought he'd gotten past during the dinner and dancing.

She paused in front of her door after retrieving her key from the little bag she carried, and turned to face him. "Thank you for a very nice evening, Marcus." Although she met his eyes, her smile was an impersonal social expression that annoyed the hell out of him. He *knew* she had felt the chemistry—or whatever it was called—between them.

He stepped a little closer, invading her personal space, and her eyes widened fractionally before she could control her reaction. "Sylvie, will you go out with me again tomorrow night?"

She took a deep breath. "I'm not sure that's wise, Marcus. You own a company that's trying to swallow my employer in one big bite. It makes me uncomfortable—"

"I want to see you again," he interrupted, "and you want to see me. Don't you?"

She hesitated. "I—"

He put a finger over her lips, stopping himself from probing the inside of that soft, lush mouth with an act of will. "No lying."

"I wasn't going to lie," she said against his finger. "But I think it's a bad idea to mix business with—"

"This doesn't have a damn thing to do with business," he growled. He took her arms and pulled her against him, lowering his head to find her mouth in the same instant.

She gave one startled squeak and he could feel the resistance in her rigid posture. But as he covered her lips with his and stroked his palms over her back, she relaxed and began to kiss him back, soft clinging kisses that invited more. And more. The feel of her mouth moving under his was so erotic that it was all he could do to keep from plunging his tongue between her lips and seeking out the sweet responsiveness he knew was there. But he didn't want to frighten her and she hadn't yet opened her mouth to him. She was an odd blend of cool sophistication and wide-eyed innocence. The way she kissed surprised him. He'd expected her to be a lot more experienced.

They still wore their coats, though each had undone the buttons in deference to the building's warmth. With slow, definite movements, he pulled aside the heavy fabrics so that her slender body shifted against him, brushing the ridge of swelling flesh behind his zipper. Boldly, he pressed her against the arousal he couldn't hide, letting her feel what she did to him.

With a small sound of dismay, she pulled herself out of his arms, staring at him with wide, shocked eyes.

"Wow." He ran his hands up and down the wool fabric that covered her back, refusing to let her go though she braced her palms against his chest and wedged her arms between them so he couldn't pull her close again. "That didn't feel businesslike to me."

"It didn't feel *smart,* either," she retorted, making him smile. Damn, but she was a quick thinker, even when he'd clearly just rattled her.

Then she sighed. She lifted one small hand and laid it along his jaw.

Without thinking, he turned his head and pressed a hot kiss into her palm, letting the very tip of his tongue caress her. "Say yes," he whispered against the soft flesh. "Come out with me tomorrow night."

She hesitated for so long he'd already started to marshal more arguments. He lifted her hand from his mouth and laid his lips over the fleshy pad of her thumb and on down to her wrist, where he could feel a wild pulse thrumming a rapid pattern.

Then he heard her soft sigh, as if all her arguments had flown off into space, gone forever. "Yes," she whispered.

He wanted to leap into the air and yell, "All right!" and then carry her off to his cave, a notion that would probably have appalled her independent spirit if she'd known. He settled for pressing one final swift kiss on her full lips. "Great," he said. "I'll pick you up at seven. Dress casual."

"Where will we be going?"

"Dress casual," he repeated. He stepped back and turned to leave before he gave in to the urge to devour her.

"Marcus?" He voice was strangely tentative. "You're not—you won't do anything to harm Colette tomorrow, will you?"

What was one day in the grand scheme of things? "No." He made the pledge easily. "I promise nothing will happen tomorrow."

But as he walked down the steps to the door of 20 Amber Court, he was aware of a small pocket of discontent hidden within the sensual glow he still felt. It rankled that she felt she had to use herself to bargain for Colette, a company that surely didn't deserve a treasure like Sylvie Bennett.

Sylvie leaned against the inside of her apartment door, one hand lifted to her mouth. Now *that* wasn't like anything she'd ever experienced before. Her fingers lightly explored her lips, which still tingled and throbbed from Marcus's kisses. Any man that could kiss like that should be declared a threat to national security.

She sighed and started walking toward her bedroom. Her body still sang where she'd been clasped against him.

The stunning amber brooch that Rose had lent her that morning lay on her dresser and she touched it with an idle finger. As she did, she suddenly remembered a conversation from a few weeks earlier, when Rose had invited Sylvie to her apartment for Thanksgiving dinner. Three of Sylvie's friends and co-workers had been there. The women all lived at Amber Court and were especially close to Rose, who clearly delighted in her role as surrogate mother. Recently, all three of her friends had married or become engaged and one of them, Meredith Blair, had made a joke about the brooch, which she had been wearing at the meal.

"Better watch out, Sylvie," Meredith teased. *"If Rose*

*loans you this brooch, you can kiss your single days
goodbye. I was wearing that the day I met Adam and
Rose loaned it to Jayne the day she met Erik. I think that
whoever made it must have put a love spell on it.''*

''You're kidding!'' Lila Maxwell's engagement ring
sparkled as she automatically lifted a hand to pat her
breast where the pin would be placed. *''And I was wearing it the day Nick and I...''* She trailed off, her cheeks
glowing with heated color.

Nick Camden laid one large hand over his fiancée's
and his blue eyes gleamed as he stepped into the amused
silence. *''The day I first realized I couldn't live without
her.''*

Rose was beaming, her gaze knowing. *''Perhaps there
is something magical about it.''* She'd turned to Sylvie.
''I guess I'd better loan it to you one day.''

''That's all right,'' Sylvie said hastily. *''I like my life
just the way it is, thank you.''*

But when she'd run into Rose in the hallway this morning as she was racing to work, her mind had been on the
board meeting she'd been determined to invade. She'd
remembered the brooch but not the conversation—until
now.

As she took off her things and put them away, her eyes
kept returning to the sparkling pin lying atop the dresser.
Could it be...? Oh, how ridiculous could she get! Of
course not.

But still...Jayne, Lila and Meredith *had* all met the
loves of their lives while wearing it. What if she and
Marcus...? The warmth that lingered from his touch in-
tensified. He was the perfect man, except for that one
little flaw regarding Colette. They shared common interests and she found him more attractive than any man
she'd ever met.

Right. And she'd known him for less than a day. *You have some major hots for Mr. Marcus Grey,* she warned herself. *It has nothing to do with how compatible you are—except in the most physical sense.* Which was exactly why she hadn't invited him in tonight. She'd never had a problem ending an evening before. In fact, if she'd ever exchanged more than a perfunctory good-night peck at the end of a first date, she couldn't remember it. The sole intimate relationship she'd had had occurred during one of her more extended runaway excursions. She'd been sixteen. The experience had been painful and significantly less than romantic and she'd never been eager to repeat it with anyone else...until now.

She shook her head, annoyed with herself. Heaven only knew what Marcus thought of her easy acquiescence to his kisses. He probably was planning her seduction, and who could blame him? A little shiver ran through her as her vivid imagination conjured up images to go with that last thought.

What would she have done if he'd pressed her? She shuddered as a small thrill ran through her, wishing she could be sure she would have sent him away. But in his arms, she doubted she could be responsible for her own actions.

Which was why she should stay far, far away from him.

So what had she done? Accepted a date for the following evening. Oh, she could lie to herself and say that she'd had the best interests of Colette at heart, but what was the point? She'd never felt before as Marcus made her feel, never thought her life was incomplete without a man. Until tonight, when she'd laughed with him, when she'd been soothed by the quiet understanding in his eyes when she'd spoken of her childhood, when she'd gone into his arms on the dance floor and suddenly felt like she'd come home.

It was a powerfully seductive feeling for a girl who'd gone most of her life without understanding or affection. She could look objectively at herself and see what she'd made of her life: she'd come from reveling in being an outcast to reaching for success with both hands. She'd made friends, an accomplishment of note considering the rebellious, defensive teen she'd been. Now she shared warm, caring friendships with a number of people, including Rose, whom she'd come to love like a mother.

But she'd never met a man who had made her feel that she was missing part of herself when he wasn't with her.

Good grief, girl! She grimaced at herself in the mirror as she finished brushing her teeth. *You've had one date. One date! Nothing to get excited about.*

But in her dreams she danced in the warm embrace of a tall man with green eyes, a man who fit the missing piece of the puzzle that was Sylvie Bennett.

She floated around the office the next day. Her boss, Wil Hughes, looked at her strangely after her screensaver kicked in for the third time while they were working on a new ad campaign.

"What's on your mind, Sylvie? You seem a little distracted today."

"Sorry." She moved the mouse and the screen switched back to her program. "I'm just worried about what Grey Enterprises is trying to do."

Wil nodded. "We all are. But there's nothing we can do but wait until the ax falls and then see what our options are." He ran a distracted hand over the silvering hair at his temple. "Lord, I hate the thought of leaving Colette and starting again somewhere else."

"Maybe it won't come to that."

"Maybe." Wil sounded doubtful. Then he grinned. "Since we're talking about Grey, tell me exactly what happened when you dragged the lion out of his lair yesterday." He shook his head as if he couldn't quite believe what she'd done. "Did you get anywhere?"

Sylvie smiled, recalling Wil's half-hearted, obligatory dressing down for what she'd done. "It was more a case of the lion dragging me. And I don't have any idea if I made any headway changing his mind. We went to dinner last night, though, and I'm seeing him again tonight, so I'll keep working on our behalf."

Her boss sat up straighter. "Are you kidding me?"

Sylvie shook her head. "Not one little bit."

"Holy cow. Maeve will wet her drawers when I tell her. You'll have to come over for dinner soon and give her every detail."

"I'd love to. Come to dinner, that is," she added hastily. She smiled impudently. "The details might have to be censored."

Wil chuckled. "Maeve will worm them out of you."

Maeve, Wil's wife, was confined to a wheelchair thanks to an auto accident several years earlier, and suffered from chronic health problems. Despite her ailments, Maeve was a warm and lively woman. She and Wil had been two of Sylvie's first friends when she'd come to Colette, long before Sylvie had been transferred to marketing. Sylvie would do anything for them. She knew one of Wil's biggest worries about the takeover was how he would find insurance to pay for Maeve's constant health crises if he were let go. "How's she doing?"

"Pretty well. Her doctor feels she's recovered completely from that bout of flu."

Sylvie put her hand on his and squeezed it comfortingly. "I'm glad to hear that."

The office door opened then and they both turned to see who it was. But they couldn't tell. A huge flower arrangement in a stunning holiday design topped a green wool skirt that gave way to a shapely pair of legs.

"Where's the desk?" Lila Maxwell's voice issued from behind the flowers.

Sylvie laughed as she quickly rose and guided her friend to a table. "Put them right over here. What are you doing acting as a delivery girl?"

Lila deposited the arrangement on the table and her dark eyes sparkled as she straightened. "I was on my way up from downstairs when I saw these. The girls in reception said they were for you so I said I'd bring them up. I'm dying to see who they're from!"

"Bet I can guess," said Wil.

Sylvie reached for the small white envelope accompanying the flowers and tore it open. *Looking forward to seeing you this evening. Marcus.*

"Well, well, well. Looks like you made quite an impression." Lila was shamelessly peering over her shoulder, reading the message and Wil was right behind her. "Rose told me you went out with him last night. Must have been a hit since you're going for a repeat."

Sylvie felt warmth creeping up her neck. "We had a nice time," she said cautiously.

"Do us all a favor," Wil suggested. "Have a nice time again tonight and while you're at it, talk him out of closing Colette."

Sylvie grimaced. "Sounds like prostitution, doesn't it?"

Both her friends looked genuinely shocked. Lila was the first to recover. "Sylvie, you're not going out with him just to try to help the company, are you? From the sound of his reputation, you wouldn't make a dent.''

Sylvie smiled, trying to ignore the small voice that urged her to leap to Marcus's defense. ''No. Last night I went out with him to try to help the company. Tonight, I'm going out with him because he's a great dancer and we had a lovely evening last night. No big deal.''

Three

***

As Sylvie dressed in navy wool trousers and a lighter blue silk sweater that evening, she knew that this night *was* a big deal, though she'd assured her friends otherwise. She had a huge ball of nerves clutching at her stomach and she rarely, if ever, felt nervous about dates. Would he still hold the same appeal he'd had for her last night? Or would she laugh at herself and chalk up her silly dreams to too much wine and dancing?

The doorbell rang as she was tidying up her living room. When she opened the door, Marcus straightened from a lounging position against the doorframe. She met his piercing emerald eyes—

And felt the ball of nerves in her stomach drop straight to her toes. Her heart skipped a beat; her breath caught in her throat.

Lord, but he was beautiful. He wore black, fine-wale corduroy trousers and a white shirt with the neck unbuttoned beneath a black bomber jacket. A swatch of golden curls peeked from the open vee. His shoulders looked as wide as her doorway though she knew it was only an illusion.

"Good evening." She was amazed that her voice sounded so normal.

"Good evening. You look lovely." His eyes raked over her.

"Thank you. And thank you for the flowers you sent today." She indicated the mantel above her fireplace, where the arrangement reigned in stately splendor. "As you can see, they're quite striking." She took a houndstooth wool jacket from the closet and he reached for it, holding it so that she could turn and slip it on. Her back was to him as she placed her arms in the sleeves and as he lifted it over her shoulders, he wrapped his arms around her and drew her back against his body.

"Sylvie," he murmured. "I've waited for this all day."

She put her hands up to his brawny forearms, though she didn't try to get away. They both wore coats but it still was a sweet torture to be held so closely against his lean frame. A torture she knew she had to resist.

She kept her head bent, reminding herself yet again that she was *not* the kind of woman who fell into bed with a man after a single date. Or even several of them. "About last night," she said, and her voice sounded breathless, even to her own ears, "I don't…that is, I'm not the kind of girl who—"

"I never thought you were." There was a tender sort of amusement in his tone. His arms tightened for a moment and she had the feeling he was fighting some internal battle. But then he released her and took her hand, turning her toward the door. "Ready to go?"

He was driving the same low-slung black Mercedes coupe he had driven last night. And like last night, he drove north along the shore of Lake Michigan. But unlike last night, he didn't stop at the Youngsville Country Club. Instead, he kept moving for another twenty minutes.

When he finally pulled off the lakeshore drive, they were at a beautiful little Italian restaurant of which she'd heard. It fronted a wide sandy beach that looked out over the lake. The maître d' led them to a table in a secluded corner.

After perusing the wine list and making a selection, Marcus settled back and regarded her with an intensity that she found somewhat unnerving. "So. Where did we leave off last night?"

The exact memory of where they'd left off the evening before rushed her head. Caught off guard, she blushed.

He grinned, and she caught her breath at the sheer sensual beauty of him. "A penny for your thoughts."

"Not a chance." She shook her head, smiling back as she made an effort to steady her voice and sound normal. "Let's see…I think you'd decided I wasn't really re-formed before we hit the dance floor."

He nodded. "Tell me more about this group home you went to. What made you decide to shape up?"

Sylvie smiled as fond memories swept over her. "That's easy. A hug."

His eyebrows lifted. "A hug?"

She nodded. "I was a surly brat who was determined to paddle in the opposite direction of the current for the first few weeks I was there. But there was this lady…a volunteer who came to the home twice a week. She tutored kids who needed extra help, pitched in at mealtime if the staff was shorthanded, played cards and stuff with the rest of the kids sometimes. The first time she met me, she came right up and hugged me and said, "It's lovely to meet you, Sylvie."

Marcus looked a little skeptical. "You must not have been too hard a nut to crack if that's all it took."

"Oh, she didn't get through right away," Sylvie said. "But after the first few weeks passed, I realized I was starting to look forward to those hugs. One day I got an A on a math test. It was more of an accident than anything else, but she was so delighted you'd have thought I got into the National Honor Society. She hugged me and congratulated me and told me how proud she was of me. Then she told me I must be proud of myself...and I realized I was. That was pretty much the beginning of the 'new me.'"

He was studying her. "She must have been quite a lady."

"She is. She still goes to the home twice a week. I go with her once a month." She smiled fondly. "You met her yesterday."

"Mrs. Carson?" His shoulders straightened a bit and his eyes came alert. "Your, ah, landlady?"

"One and the same." She wondered why he seemed so interested in that bit of trivia, but as the server arrived with the wine he'd ordered, she forgot the moment.

They chatted easily over dinner and he asked her about her work. "So what does the Assistant Director of Marketing do, exactly?"

She shrugged. "Pretty much what you'd expect. I oversee teams that work on designing promotions, ad campaigns and slogans for the company. Right now we're working on next year's autumn advertising budget."

"Nine months from now?"

She nodded. "It takes a while to pull together a really outstanding marketing plan. We usually work that far ahead. By Valentine's Day, I'll be thinking about Christmas again."

He chuckled. "Hard to keep your seasons straight, I'd think." Then he gestured out the window. "Speaking of seasonal things, I suspect we're going to have a white Christmas this year."

She glanced in the direction he indicated. Large, fluffy snowflakes were pelting down over the moon-silvered lake in a heavy swirling cloud. "Oh, good!" She clapped her hands together. "I love snow." Except, of course, when she had important, early morning meetings.

"I didn't realize they were calling for snow tonight."

The waiter, who had returned to clear away their dishes, overheard his comment. "It's supposed to be the second major storm of the season, sir."

Marcus grimaced. "Great. And I'm driving a toy car." He leaned across the table toward Sylvie. "I hate to cut this evening short, but the Mercedes doesn't handle well on slippery roads. We'd better start back."

She nodded, a little disappointed. "All right."

Marcus paid the bill and retrieved their coats. As they stepped out of the sheltered warmth of the restaurant, a fierce gust of wind from the lake caught them full in the face.

Already the ground was covered and the sidewalk was getting slick. Marcus grunted in annoyance. "Stay here," he told her. "I'll bring the car around."

She did as he instructed and within moments they were heading cautiously out of the parking lot along the lake road back toward Youngsville. They didn't speak much. There was enough snow obscuring the road that Marcus needed to keep all his attention on his driving. Even so, the trip that had taken them just a shade over half an hour going out took them more than twice that returning. The plows and cinder trucks were keeping the freeway around the city open but when Marcus got off at Sylvie's exit, the coupe slid down the small hill and right through the stop sign at the bottom of the off-ramp. The sports car spun halfway around as he grimly pumped the pedal to keep the brakes from locking and worked the wheel to compensate for the spin without sending them into a ditch.

He cursed vividly as the wheels, seeking traction, began to spin on the ever more slippery road, but he got the car headed in the right direction. "It's a good thing there wasn't anyone coming through that intersection."

Sylvie nodded, her heart still pounding and her adrenaline rushing.

"I'm sorry." His voice was sincere. "I didn't listen to the forecast. I wasn't expecting a snow like this."

"I heard one earlier this afternoon," she said. "They were calling for a light snow with an inch or two of accumulation. Nothing like this." She waved a hand at the white world beyond the snug interior of the sports car.

They traveled the rest of the way to her apartment without incident, though the car slipped and skidded as the tires tried in vain to find purchase on the snow-covered roads. When Marcus finally eased the car into a parking space in the lot behind Amber Court, his sigh of relief was audible.

As he escorted Sylvie into the building, she noticed that the snow seemed to be falling even harder. This looked like a genuine blizzard in the making and suddenly she was worried about Marcus getting home. Although she didn't know exactly where he lived, she'd

read that his custom-built home was in an exclusive en-
clave called Cedar Forest, which was northwest of the
city. Which meant another drive of at least twenty
minutes under normal conditions for him. Tonight...heaven knew how long it would take.

"Would you like to come in?" she asked as they approached her apartment door. "I could turn on the
weather channel so you could see what they're predict-
ing."

Marcus snorted. "I don't need to see the weather channel to tell me I'm going to have a hell of a time getting
home in this."

She hesitated. "You—you're welcome to stay the
night. It's not safe to drive." It wasn't the safest thing
she'd ever done, but she couldn't send him out on the
roads again in good conscience.

Beside her, Marcus stopped in the act of unwinding a
black-and-red tartan scarf from around his neck. Slowly,
his gaze came to hers and the heat she saw there made
her shiver in automatic feminine response. "I'm not sure
that's a good idea."

"I'm not, either," she said honestly. "But it would be
heartless to send you back out in that weather. By morning it should have stopped and the roads should be
clear." She cleared her throat. "My sofa pulls out into a
bed."

He smiled then, lightening the dark intensity in his
eyes. "Will my feet hang off the end?"

She shook her head as she fished out her key and un-
locked the door. "I doubt it. It's a queen mattress. And
if it's not big enough, you can have my bed and I'll take
the couch."

"No." Marcus followed her inside and closed her door

behind them, flicking home the dead bolt. "The only way I plan to sleep in your bed is with you there next to me."

The heat flared, lodging in her abdomen. She ignored it, saying in the firmest voice she could manage, "I'm not going to sleep with you, Marcus. I thought we'd established that."

He shrugged out of his jacket and hung it and the scarf on the doorknob of her closet. "Plans change." His eyes were gleaming. "Besides, I never agreed to any such thing."

She opened her mouth to fire back a blast, but abruptly she realized he was teasing her. His words triggered another train of thought as she put her own coat away and headed for the kitchen. "Have you thought any more about your plans for Colette, Inc.?"

The good humor fell away from his face, leaving an expressionless mask in its place. She was sorry the moment the words left her mouth. She was growing to like him, perhaps more than she should, and she didn't want to ruin the evening.

"I think about Colette all the time." His answer was cryptic.

She hadn't intended to pursue it but she couldn't stop. It was, after all, the whole reason she'd met him in the first place. She turned from the cupboard where she'd been in the act of taking down two coffee mugs. "In what way?"

He shrugged. "How best to integrate it with my current holdings. That sort of thing."

"But...but you *can't*. Marcus, you simply can't dissolve Colette!" Her voice rose in agitation as she set the mugs on the counter. "Can you tell me there won't be personnel cuts if there's a merger?"

He crossed his arms, making his biceps bulge beneath

the fine cotton of his white shirt. As he leaned back against her counter, his eyes were narrow and bright while he studied her. "I can't make you any promises."

There was a decisive note in his tone and she frowned as she ground coffee with quick, efficient movements and prepared her machine. "Can't, or won't?"

He straightened from his position and came across the small space toward her. She whirled to face the cabinets, her hands clenched on the edge of the counter. But he came on anyhow, setting his big hands on her shoulders and gently squeezing as he lowered his head and spoke into her ear. "Either. Both. Take your pick." His grip tightened and he turned her inexorably around. "I don't want to talk business with you, Sylvie."

She gazed up at him, her eyes bright with tears, and the passion she felt for her employer rang in her voice when she spoke again. "I can't separate my life into easy little compartments like you can." She ducked beneath his arm and headed for the bedroom. "I'm going to pack a few things. I'll stay downstairs with Rose tonight. You can have my bed."

She didn't dare turn and look at him as she fled to her bedroom.

Marcus tossed and turned on Sylvie's sofa bed, finally waking for good after an endlessly long night. He supposed it was stupid, but he'd meant what he'd said about not sleeping in her bed without her. Though it was still dark, the illuminated light on his watch told him it was nearly six-thirty.

After six in the morning, and he was alone in Sylvie's apartment. Damn! He had a lot of plans for spending the night at her place, but sleeping alone on a lumpy sofa bed wasn't one of them. With a muttered curse, he rose and grabbed the towels she had so thoughtfully provided and turned on her shower, then stood beneath the driving spray, wishing the water could sluice away all his problems with this merger.

Merger. In his heart, he knew that wasn't quite what he intended. Colette would cease to exist once he was through absorbing the jewelry manufacturing into his holdings. Grey Gems, a division of Grey Enterprises, or something like that.

It's just business, he defended himself. *A sound economic move. Colette's been faltering lately. The Grey name will boost the stock again.*

He conveniently ignored the fact that rumors about Grey acquiring Colette were what had driven the stock down in the first place. Not his fault. He hadn't started the rumors. Though he had to admit he hadn't done anything to squelch them, either. And then Colette had lodged that ridiculous lawsuit against Grey.

And lost. Because they hadn't been able to prove, as he'd known they wouldn't, that he'd had anything to do with those rumors.

He almost wished he *had* thought of starting a rumor. It had been an incredibly effective tool for his plans. Several jittery investors had actually contacted him before he ever got to them to offer a buyout!

Thinking of buyouts and investors made him think of work. He needed to get home to change before he went to work this morning. Which reminded him of why he was here in this apartment instead of in his own spacious home.

He dressed and stalked to the window, brushing aside Sylvie's elegant drapes to stare at the white world outside. Though Youngsville didn't get as much snow as portions of the state farther inland from the Great Lakes, there had to be close to a foot of snow on the ground. It was still snowing lightly. But the street beyond the parking lot was plowed and he imagined most everything else would be, too. Not perfect, but surely good enough for him to get the Mercedes home and take a more suitable vehicle to his office.

He flicked on the television and watched the weather channel long enough to learn that there would be more snow tonight. A typical Indiana winter appeared to have begun with a vengeance.

In the kitchen, he reheated the coffee Sylvie hadn't stayed to drink last night. It was stale but so was his mood. He had just finished and was taking his coat from her closet door when a key scraped in her lock and the door swung open. Sylvie stepped quietly into the room, stopping when she saw him.

"Good morning." He kept his voice pleasant and non-committal.

"Good morning." She looked lovely, as always. She'd obviously taken clothes with her because she was dressed for work in a striking lavender suit that made her ivory skin and exotic coloring leap out at him. She also looked…troubled.

"About last night," she said.

He sighed, holding up a hand. "I know you want me to—"

"No."

He stopped and stared at her.

"I realize it isn't fair of me to make demands on you regarding your business." She took a deep breath. "I'm sorry I got angry last night. Just…please, if you can, look carefully at each person on the staff before you start cutting. There are a lot of wonderful people working there who don't deserve to be axed because of an old grudge."

"It's not an old grudge," he said impatiently, though a little voice in his head asked, *Oh, yeah?* "It's business." But he couldn't resist those enormous puppy eyes pleading with him. "I promise to be very careful when—and if—there are personnel decisions to be made."

She closed her eyes for a moment. "Thank you," she whispered.

He stepped toward her, reaching out and pulling her into his arms. "I thought you were never going to speak to me again," he said roughly, a little shaken by how relieved he was to have her doing just that. He cradled her chin in one hand and lifted her mouth for his kiss.

She shook her head before he could capture her mouth. "If I were smart," she said, "I wouldn't. But I guess I'm not very smart because I couldn't stay away."

"I'm glad." He did kiss her then, claiming her mouth possessively in a deep, stirring exchange that fired his loins and threatened his self-control so that he had to set her away from him. "Tomorrow night," he said, "I have tickets for a play at the Ingalls Park Theatre. Come with me."

She nodded. "All right."

He left her then, heading for home and then his office, satisfied with the way things were progressing between them.

His arm was draped around her shoulders as they sat in his private box at the theater the following evening, watching a beautifully staged production of Dickens's *A Christmas Carol.* And though she tried mightily to keep her mind on the play, Marcus's nearness, his warm, firm body so close to hers, distracted her time and time again. His palm cupped her shoulder and his thumb lazily grazed the side of her neck where it was bared by her evening dress.

She should despise herself for her weakness. She should show some backbone and resist temptation. She should never be contemplating getting involved with him. But it was already too late for that. Like it or not, she was involved.

And if she was honest with herself, she did like it. A lot. She hadn't dated a tremendous amount in her twenty-seven years. In high school and college, after she'd become less troubled and more focused, she'd been single-minded about her studies, and when she'd gone to work at Colette shortly after graduation, she'd thrown herself into her career wholeheartedly. She hadn't had a lot of time for men. And there hadn't been men beating down her door trying to change her mind, either. She'd come to the conclusion that she was too…she didn't quite know what to call it. Self-sufficient? Intelligent? Strong-willed? A little of all of those, perhaps. The men she had dated were frequently one-shot wonders who hadn't called a second time. And she supposed it was telling that she hadn't cared enough to be hurt by the rejection.

If Marcus never called again, she'd care. She'd be hurt.

Marcus made her feel…different things. Things she'd never felt before in her entire life. And not just physical things, though God knew she certainly felt those! Something within her recognized something in him, recognized and reached out, though she couldn't define or control it. She thought of Rose's brooch, bending her head to see it on her dress. Maybe it *had* brought them together.

Silly, she reminded herself. *That's just a silly superstition.* Still…he was right for her in a way she'd never known before. She wasn't willing to set that aside lightly.

Marcus was a very good man. She knew it. And she was sure he would change his mind about Colette eventually.

As the play ended, he helped her into her long evening coat and escorted her down the stairs, where they joined the crowd flowing out of the theater.

"Would you like to get a drink?" He spoke in her ear.

She shuddered at the feel of his hot breath against the sensitive flesh there. "Yes." If the evening never ended, she'd be quite content.

He took her hand and led her through the crowd. They walked around the corner to a brightly lit little pub, where they settled into a booth against the wall. Marcus ordered wine for them both and she excused herself to find the ladies' room.

When she returned, there was a tall man with striking silver hair standing beside the table talking to Marcus. Marcus rose as she approached.

"Sylvie, I'd like you to meet Kenneth Vance. Ken's the managing director of the Ingalls Park Theatre. Ken, Ms. Sylvie Bennett."

"It's a pleasure to meet you, Ms. Bennett."

"Oh!" Sylvie shook the hand the man extended. "It's *my* pleasure, Mr. Vance. We saw the show tonight. It was wonderful."

Vance smiled, inclining his head. "Thank you. But you can thank Marcus for it, as well. Without his considerable financial contributions, it would be extremely difficult to offer the caliber of professional theater that we present."

To her surprise, Marcus looked uncomfortable. "If you don't shut up, Ken, you're never getting another dime."

The actor laughed. "My lips are sealed."

A few minutes later, they climbed into the big SUV that Marcus was driving in deference to the snow.

"Hmm," she said as he handed her into the front seat. "Philanthropy. What other causes do you support?"

Marcus shrugged as he came around and climbed into the driver's seat. "Oh, you know how it is. You give a little here, you give a little there."

"Right." She eyed him with amusement, warmth spreading through her at the verification of her assessment of his character. "I suspect your idea of giving a little and mine are vastly different."

He shrugged, apparently unconcerned. "Not so different, I imagine." He picked up her hand and slid his fingers through hers. "You have a big heart."

"And you've come to that conclusion because…?" She was smiling, slightly embarrassed.

"It takes a very big heart to be so concerned for all the people you work with," he said simply. "I admire that quality in you."

It would have been the perfect opportunity to press him about Colette again. But she bit her tongue. Instead of touching on the sensitive topic, she said, "Mr. Vance is quite charming. Have you known him long?"

"For about a decade." Marcus grinned. "He's devoted to his precious theater. I think Ken would do almost anything to keep it afloat."

Much as she felt about Colette. But she didn't say it aloud, settling for, "He sounds very committed."

"He is. Actually, my mother is the one who got me involved. She was on the board for a number of years but she's been traveling more and more and she suggested I take her place."

Sylvie was instantly intrigued. It was hard to imagine Marcus with a mother, hard to imagine him as a little boy. He was so…so masculine, his personality so firmly stamped with self-confidence and determination. Had he had that kind of drive as a child? "I didn't realize your mother lived here," she said.

He grinned. "Oh, you couldn't pull that information out of the computer the other day when you went looking?"

She made a face at him. She knew from her reading that his mother was a Cobham, one of the prominent Cobhams of Chicago. But she hadn't dug any deeper than that.

"I'm a native of Youngsville," he said. "My mother's family has been in Chicago for a long time. She met my father when they literally bumped into each other at an art exhibition in the city. After they married, they settled in Youngsville."

"And started Van Arl."

"And started Van Arl," he agreed.

"Do you have any brothers or sisters?"

Marcus shook his head. "No. I'm an only child."

"Any other family in the area?"

His eyebrows rose and he turned to look at her for a second as they paused at a red light. "Are we playing Twenty Questions? When is it my turn?"

"You had your turn already," she said. "You know far more about me than I do about you."

He sighed. "True. Okay, here's the nutshell version: I have no living grandparents. My father died when I was eighteen. My mother lives a few blocks from my home in a condo complex. What else do you want to know?"

She hesitated. "I don't know—what's your favorite color?"

He laughed aloud. "Blue. Yours?"

"Red. Favorite kind of music?"

"Classical. Yours?"

"I like all kinds."

"Okay," he said. "I've got one. Do you have hobbies?"

She shook her head. "Not really. I suppose I'm a workaholic. I do like to read when I have spare time, though."

"What about activities? Favorite kinds of exercise?"

She made a face. "That's a dirty word. I love to dance, but you already know that. Skiing's fun, and I enjoy swimming. I play racquetball three times a week after work but that's more to keep in shape than because I like it."

"Racquetball, huh?" His voice was speculative. "We'll have to test each other's skill one of these days."

"Oh, no," she said hastily. "I only play for fun. You, on the other hand, are probably one of those driven people who can't stand to lose."

"I hate to be so predictable."

She patted his shoulder. "Sorry. It goes with the Type A business shark personality."

"Business shark? Is that how you see me?"

"Well," she said gently, "you didn't make your fortune working for charity or digging ditches. On the other hand, you do give some of it away to worthy causes, so you're not completely without finer qualities."

"That's a relief." His voice was dry. "Sylvie?"

"Hmm?"

"What have we accomplished with this little exercise? Other than learning a bit of completely trivial surface information about each other?"

"It's not trivial! I firmly believe in getting to know someone well before...well, before..." She'd started that sentence before she'd thought about how to end it. Now she decided there was no appropriate way to end it. "Before getting to know them any better,'' she finished lamely.

Marcus hooted with laughter. ''Now *that* was eloquent.'' They'd arrived at Amber Court and he came around to help her out of the Navigator.

But when she'd slipped down from the high seat, he didn't move away. She was caged in the space between the open car door and his tall frame and she took a deep breath, striving for dignity. ''I think you know what I mean.''

There was a moment of silence, and she felt the shimmer of an undeniable attraction stirring the air between them. Marcus set his hands at her waist and his eyes were dark in the dim light as he gazed down at her. ''Despite what you may think, I also believe in getting to know someone with whom I want to develop a deeper relationship.''

She swallowed. ''A deeper relationship?'' It was almost a squeak.

Slowly, he lifted her arms and placed them around his neck, then tugged her against him. ''Much deeper.''

Thrills of sensual delight raced through her despite the heavy coats they each wore. He molded her mouth with his, drawing her head back with one hand in her hair, then slid his mouth along her jaw to her ear, where she felt the nibble of his strong teeth on her sensitive earlobe. She shivered involuntarily but as his arms drew her even closer and his mouth traced her cheekbone, she managed to get one hand between them, covering his mouth with her palm.

''Wait.''

''I've been waiting,'' he growled against her hand. ''If I'd followed my instincts, we'd be in a warm bed right now.''

As he'd probably intended, the words charged the air with a new urgency. But still she resisted. "I'm not ready to sleep with you, Marcus."

"You wouldn't just be sleeping with me. Don't cheapen what's between us."

"Attraction," she threw at him. "That's what's between us. Just because I'm attracted to you doesn't mean—"

"It's more than mere physical attraction and you know it."

"I don't know that," she said stubbornly. "I'm not a good-time girl, Marcus. If it's experience and easy fun you want, you're with the wrong woman."

"That's not what I want," he said in a low voice.

"Then what is it?"

Silence hung between them again, charged with tension. She wished she could call back the impetuous words. She didn't want to sound too needy, nor did she want to push him for something he couldn't give her.

"You," he said quietly. "Just you." He released a heavy sigh and stepped back, his hands dropping away from her. "I'm no more comfortable with the way I'm feeling than you are, Sylvie. This is new ground. For both of us."

His honesty disarmed her, and warmed her. She put up a hand to his lean cheek, brushing her thumb over his chiseled lips. "I want you, too," she whispered. "I just...have to be sure."

He smiled, pressing a kiss to her thumb. "And here I thought you were the impetuous type."

She smiled back, relieved that they had cleared the tense hurdle of a moment before. "Guess you don't know me as well as you think."

"I intend to." Before she could respond, he turned her

toward the building, slipping his arm around her to shield her from the bitter wind. He escorted her to the door of her apartment, then took her in his arms once again, kissing her with restrained passion before stepping back. "I have to go out of town this weekend. But I'll call you."

Four

On Saturday, Sylvie played racquetball with Jim from Accounting at 9:00 a.m. She beat him three times in a row, though he claimed it was only because his energy level was low due to sleepless nights with his newborn daughter. After they finished, she followed him over to his house for a brief visit with his wife and baby.

She did her grocery shopping, then went home again and did her laundry while she cleaned her apartment. Late in the afternoon, she showered and dressed in casual clothes, then hit a local mall to get some more of her Christmas shopping done. As she browsed the aisles, she wondered if she should get Marcus a gift. They'd hardly known each other long enough; maybe she'd wait until closer to Christmas. Although heaven knew what one got a man with as much money as he had. A bank vault for all his loot?

She checked her answering machine the moment she

walked in the door that evening. No messages. Telling herself he'd only left that day, she squashed the deep sense of disappointment that she felt at not hearing from him.

The next morning she went to church, then took the bus to Wil and Maeve's home, where she enjoyed Wil's culinary skills and played cards with them afterward. She deliberately lingered, refusing to allow herself to be one of those pathetic women who sat by the telephone waiting for it to ring.

When she got home, the message light was blinking and she quickly punched the button, a ridiculous anticipation spreading within her. There were three messages but none of them were from Marcus. Well, she reasoned, perhaps he'd called while she was away and hadn't wanted to leave a message.

But her telephone was silent that evening, and she went to bed deflated and mildly depressed.

He didn't call on Monday. Or on Tuesday, and she hated the way she ran to check the machine every evening when she entered her apartment. She started to worry. Marcus wasn't the kind of man who would promise to call and then just forget. Had something happened to him? If not, then he wasn't the kind of man she wanted, despite the fact that she could think of nothing else *but* him. She'd seen enough of her friends' relationships to know when two people were equally committed. And in those cases where it was one-sided, things rarely went well for long.

On Wednesday, the telephone at her desk rang, as it had already a million times this week. Her mind on the results of the consumer survey in front of her, she absently lifted the handset. "Sylvie Bennett, may I help you?"

"You certainly may." The voice was deep, silky, and achingly familiar.

"Marcus! Are you all right?" she demanded.

"I'm fine." His voice sounded puzzled. "Are you?"

"No." Try as she might, she couldn't keep the hurt from her tone. "I was worried that something had happened to you. I'm not accustomed to people who don't call when they say they will."

There was a moment of silence. His voice sounded wary when he spoke again. "I'm sorry to have caused you concern. I didn't specifically say *when* I'd call, did I?"

"No." And he hadn't. She just assumed he'd meant he'd call over the weekend while he was away. To her dismay, she realized she was on the verge of tears. Abruptly, she said, "I have to go now. I have work to do."

"Wait!" He took a deep breath. "I really am sorry, Sylvie. I've been busy. I can tell you're upset. Could I take you out to dinner tonight and we'll talk about it?"

"No, thank you." She'd gotten control of herself again. "I don't think it's worth dissecting. I made a wrong assumption and for that, I apologize."

"Fine. We don't have to talk about it. But will you have dinner with me?"

"No, thank you, Marcus. I'm—I just can't." She let the words hang in the air. She didn't know what was happening here but she did know one thing: she already cared too much to get involved further with a man who clearly didn't think of her the way she thought of him.

Marcus slowly replaced the telephone on its base, then shoved his office chair away from his desk in one explosive motion. Well, hell! He *had* been busy, he thought defensively. And it wasn't like he'd made her any promises.

Oh, no? Practically the last thing you said to her was that you'd never felt like this before.

Yeah, but I also told her I wasn't comfortable with it.

He exhaled heavily, clamping down on the panicky feeling that tried to raise its head. Hearing her voice had brought home to him how desperately he wanted to be with her, and God knew he'd spent the last four days thinking of her far too much for comfort. He'd forced himself to wait, not to call and betray his neediness. He'd figured her nose would be a little out of joint. In his experience, women always got that way when they couldn't keep a man on a leash. But he'd imagined he could cajole her out of her pique over dinner.

Too late, he remembered what he should have realized much earlier. Sylvie wasn't a player. Whatever was going on in her head was exactly what she said. She was straightforward. *I want you, too. I just…have to be sure.*

Damn it all! Aggrieved, he thrust his fingers through his hair.

He liked her. He really liked her. She was unlike any woman he'd ever met. And though he wanted her desperately, he knew it was more than that.

And it scared the hell out of him. He hadn't needed anyone since he was a child. And he didn't like needing anyone now.

He should just forget about her. That would be the smart thing to do. But then another memory assailed him. *I don't…that is, I'm not the kind of girl who…*

He'd been charmed at the troubled frown that had touched her smooth brow, the pink that had risen in her cheeks. Was she really that naïve? He recalled his surprise at the way she'd kissed him that first time—as if she hadn't had a lot of practice.

But under his tutelage, she was learning fast. His blood heated as he thought of the sweet way her mouth had opened under his—and then it struck him. Now that she'd learned to kiss like that, what was to stop her from responding to another man the same way? Another man could take his place. The thought made his blood heat in an entirely different manner. God, had he screwed this up for good?

He could plainly see his error now. He'd assumed her refusal to go out with him was coyness. But it wasn't. It was self-preservation.

He spun his chair around and stared out the window at the distant horizon over the lake, shrouded in mist today. He wasn't ready to admit defeat yet. If she had feelings for him like he thought—hoped—she did, then there was a way to get to her.

It would just take a little more time than he'd planned.

She'd half expected him to call her back and try to con her. What she hadn't expected was the gift.

An hour after she'd hung up from what she'd thought was her last conversation with Marcus, a messenger arrived with a small wrapped box. Inside was a delicate golden chain from which hung a gleaming crystal charm of two ballroom dancers. In the midst of a spin, the woman's dress flared out and wrapped about her partner's legs. It was the most elegant thing she'd ever seen. And it reminded her of the wonderful, magical night she'd spent on the dance floor in Marcus's arms. The rat. That was exactly what he wanted her to remember.

She was torn between stomping into his office and tossing the gift at his thick head, or flinging herself into his arms in surrender. *Which is what he's hoping you'll do,* she thought grimly. So she did nothing.

On Thursday, another messenger appeared. This one carried a beribboned basket filled with her favorite scented cologne, a matching skin cream and bath beads in the same scent. But she restrained herself when her hand threatened to reach for the telephone.

Her co-workers didn't help. Lila wandered in and examined the necklace, then carefully fastened it around Sylvie's neck. Wil told the entire lunchroom, all of whom managed to parade by her office during the afternoon for a peek at her gifts.

Through it all, she maintained a grim-lipped silence. But on Friday, when a red cashmere scarf and matching red kid-leather gloves arrived from Chasan's, one of Youngsville's most exclusive boutiques, both Lila and Wil looked at her as if she'd lost her mind.

"Sylvie, a man does not spend this kind of money on a woman he does not care about," Wil said.

"I've become a challenge," she retorted. "He hates to lose. Besides, he has money to burn. This would mean a lot more if it were a sacrifice. He probably sent his secretary out to buy a few trinkets."

"Cynic," Lila accused, fingering the red gloves. She pointed at the dancers on the chain, then at the basket of scent. "These gifts were chosen by someone who knows you."

Sylvie had to admit her friend had a point.

"Besides," Lila leaned forward and said in a stage whisper, "Rose told me you were wearing *the brooch* when you met him, and you know what that means."

"It means you're all insane," Sylvie told her. But she was smiling. Maybe she'd been too hard on Marcus. Maybe it had been an honest error. A miscommunication.

Still, she thought as she slipped into bed that night, she'd have to think very carefully before leaping back into Marcus Grey's orbit. She could very easily wind up being a comet that got incinerated in the atmosphere.

On Saturday morning, she got up early and went to the grocery store, then played racquetball with Jim. Afterward, she came home and started her laundry while she cleaned her apartment, a routine much like she usually followed on the weekend. Sometimes she varied the order just to keep herself from getting too sick of it.

She glanced at the time, and realized she'd better get a move on. Jim and his wife Marietta wanted to do a little Christmas shopping in the afternoon and Sylvie had volunteered to watch their baby girl. She was a little nervous about watching a newborn, but Marietta had assured her they wouldn't be gone long and that baby Alisa was usually quiet and easygoing.

She was just getting ready to head for a shower when the doorbell rang. It was probably her friend Meredith who lived right below her, or one of her other neighbors. Unhurriedly, she strolled to the door and slipped off the dead bolt, then pulled it wide.

Marcus stood on the other side.

"Oh. Hello." Flustered, she stepped back. He was the last person she'd expected and she imagined it showed.

"Hello." He looked as taken aback as she felt. She resisted the urge to cross her arms over her breasts as his gaze flicked down her body and back up, taking in her exercise clothing and lingering for a moment longer than necessary in the vicinity of her chest, where she'd stripped off the hot outer layers and now wore only a black sports bra. "Um, would you like to come in?"

He nodded, unsmiling, and his green eyes sharpened

as they scrutinized her face. "Please." He stepped past her and then turned as she shut the door and leaned against it.

"I don't have much time because I have plans this afternoon," she said. Oh, God, she looked awful. Only steely self-control kept her from reaching up and pulling out the rubber band securing her disheveled ponytail. She took a deep breath. "Thank you for all the lovely things you sent, but I really can't accept them."

"You can't return them," he said curtly.

"Why not?" She tried to keep her voice light and level but even she could hear the quaver of hurt in her tone. "Don't you keep your receipts?"

"Sylvie…" Marcus appeared to be searching for the right words. The mantle of self-confidence he normally wore had slipped a bit and there was something vulnerable in his eyes, something that made her hesitate and listen. "I'd like to apologize again for not calling you while I was away—"

"It's all right, Marcus. You were under no obligation—" She was *not* going to be a sucker for a smooth-talker, she admonished herself.

"Yes," he said over her objection. "I was. It may not have been spoken, but it was implied. You deserved more consideration than I showed you." He looked away. "I thought of you. Too much. And…I was bothered that I couldn't get you out of my head. It made me nervous."

"Well, consider me gone," she said quietly, though her heart had leaped at his admission. "You don't have to think of me anymore."

"But I do," he said. He didn't move, but she saw his shoulders tense. "I can't stop thinking of you. Please, Sylvie, don't write me off because I made a mistake. I want another chance."

Another chance. She was a person who'd been given a second chance and it had made a world of difference. How could she deny him the opportunity to correct his mistake as well? Especially when he combined his plea with that pathetic, no-hope-left expression. *And* the admission that he'd thought of her.

She permitted herself a small smile. "Now that sounds more like the man I know. I want this, I need that. Bring me this, do that."

He scowled, his normal arrogance returning. "I'm not that bad."

"No," she agreed, "You're not."

"So, will you go out with me this evening?"

"I can't," she said regretfully. "I have plans."

"What are you doing tonight? Another date?"

"Yes." She laughed at the expression on his face. "Not really. I just couldn't resist yanking your chain." She ignored his low growl. "I'm going skiing with a group of people from my church. We have a sort of club each winter—I got us reduced rates and a package deal on Saturday nights."

"Why am I not surprised you were the negotiator?" he asked rhetorically. Then his eyes brightened. "Would you mind if I tagged along? I enjoy skiing, though I haven't done much of it in the past few years."

Pleasure exploded within her at the thought of spending the evening with him. "That would be great, if you don't mind going in a group."

"A group is fine, as long as you're in it."

Four hours later, he was mounting the stairs to her fourth floor apartment again. Although he had left most of his heavy ski layers in the Navigator, he was wearing enough that the warmth of the building was uncomfortable and he pulled off his sweater as he walked.

Even before he got to her door, he heard the screaming baby. He looked around as he passed, wondering which apartment the unhappy infant was in, but as he approached the end of the hallway where Sylvie's door was, the decibel level of the howling increased. As he rang the bell, he concluded that the noise had to be coming from within.

When Sylvie opened the door, the immediate increase in the screaming hit him full in the face. She was carrying a tiny infant in one arm as she beckoned him to enter with a desperate look on her face.

"My friend Jim and his wife had some shopping to do," she told him above the baby's fussing. "Alisa is only four weeks old and this is the first time they've left her."

"And maybe the last, too," he observed, eyeing the baby's red face.

She grimaced. "She was fine until a few minutes ago. I'm sure she's hungry, but I can't feed her, if you get my drift. Jim and Marietta had planned to be back before her next feeding but they had to detour around an accident. They called a little while ago. They should be here any minute but I'd hate for them to hear her like this. I must have been crazy to agree to this. I've never baby-sat a newborn before in my entire life!"

That was vintage Sylvie, as he was quickly coming to know. Doing things for other people despite the fact that it might not be the best course of action for her to take. Sort of like the day they'd met, in fact. He cast the baby another wary glance. "Want me to take her?"

Her chocolate eyes widened. "Are you kidding? What do you know about babies?"

"Not much. But she can't get any more upset." He reached for the squalling infant, sliding one hand beneath the tiny skull and the other cupping the fragile body. "My office assistant has five grandchildren who have been in and out of the office since they were born. One day, her daughter-in-law had to take her preschooler to the hospital for stitches, and Doris and I got stuck with the three-month-old twins. It was learn or die that day." He held the baby up in front of his face. "Hey there," he said, "what's all this noise about?"

Alisa's little body stilled and she stopped in midshriek, her eyes fastened on his face.

"Well," said Sylvie. She sounded put out. "Go figure."

"It's my natural charm," he told her, though he kept his voice and attention on the baby. "Works every time."

"Uh-huh." She rolled her eyes in disgust, then turned and reached for something, holding it out to him. "Here, I couldn't get her to take this when she was screaming but maybe she'll accept it now."

He took the rubber pacifier from Sylvie's hand, feeling awkward as he turned the baby to settle her in the crook of one arm. She was squeaking and squirming now, and he was pretty sure another scream wasn't far away, so he held the pacifier to the tiny rosebud lips, gently moving it back and forth as he dropped his voice to a low croon. "Here you go. Why don't you suck on this for a while? I know it's not as good as your mama but it's all we've got."

To his great relief, the infant took the nipple into her mouth and began to suck lustily, moving the pacifier up and down vigorously with her eyes still fastened on his face. "So," he said to Sylvie, keeping the same low, intimate tone in which he'd been addressing the baby, "why haven't you ever been around babies? I thought all girls baby-sat."

"Stereotypical comment," she said. "I was raised in an orphanage where we were grouped by age. And I already told you what a handful I was as a foster child. Who would have wanted me looking after their kids?"

"But you straightened out."

"Not until I was nearly sixteen years old. And by then I was living in a group home for troubled kids. Not the kind of place people come to hire baby-sitters."

He nodded, realizing anew how bleak her childhood must have been. The baby squealed sharply, and he returned his attention to her, rocking her in one arm as he spoke. "That's my girl. You're just a wonderful, beautiful girl." He kept talking, aware that every time he fell silent the baby's sucking stopped or slowed altogether.

Sylvie was scurrying around the room, picking up baby blankets and extra diapers and wipes and replacing things in the capacious diaper bag that sat on her dining table. "Thank you," she said. "I didn't think I'd have any trouble with her, but as I said, my friends are a little later than they thought they'd be."

As if in response, the doorbell rang. She fairly flew across the room to answer it and the moment she opened the door, a small plump woman made a beeline for him.

"Hi there," she said, "I'm Marietta. I hope she hasn't been fussing. We got caught in traffic."

"She hasn't been very happy," Sylvie confessed. "She was trying to eat my shirt until Marcus showed up. Apparently his way with women extends to the smallest members of our sex." Her voice was rueful but she was smiling.

Marcus handed the baby to Marietta and the moment Alisa recognized her, she immediately began to get agitated again, banging her little head against her mother's chest in a futile search for dinner.

Marietta gave Marcus a distracted smile, then looked back at Sylvie. "Would you mind if I fed her here before we leave? Otherwise, she's liable to scream the whole way home."

"Not at all," said Sylvie hastily. "You can use my bedroom."

Marietta nodded, rapidly moving down the hall to the door Sylvie indicated. As Sylvie pulled the door shut and walked back toward the men, Marcus became aware that her friend Jim was staring at him strangely.

"Hello," he said, stepping forward and offering his hand.

"I'm sorry," Sylvie said. "We didn't get around to introductions, did we? Marcus, this is Jim Marrell. Jim, Marcus Grey."

Jim reached for his hand slowly, as if he were a bit dazed. "I recognized you," he said. His handshake was brief and unmemorable.

"Marcus is joining my ski club on the slopes tonight," Sylvie said brightly. "I'm hoping for a chance to push him off the mountain before he can close down Colette."

"Sylvie!" Jim looked appalled. "She's kidding, Mr. Grey. She only meant—"

"I understand that all of you are concerned about Colette," Marcus said. "It's only natural. Is that where you two met?" He'd deal with Sylvie later, he decided. Little witch, putting him on the hot seat when she knew he wouldn't retaliate.

"Yes. We work together," said Sylvie.

"Well, uh, not exactly together," Jim clarified. "I'm in accounting, Sylvie's in marketing. We actually met at the water cooler."

"Ah. The good old water cooler."

Jim's eyes darted toward the hall. "I'd better go check on Marietta. I'll be right back." He skirted Marcus cautiously, then practically sprinted down the hallway and disappeared into the room where his wife had gone.

Sylvie's eyebrows rose as she looked after him. "What did you say to him while I was gone?"

"Nothing."

"Then why is he acting like you're the Big Bad Wolf and he's Little Red Riding Hood?"

Marcus shrugged. "If everyone in your company is repeating the same stories you threw at me when we met, it's no wonder he's nervous. The guy probably thinks he's going to lose his job if he's rude to me…unlike some other people I could name."

Sylvie merely smiled angelically. "I'll get my things and we can go. Jim and Mari can lock the door on their way out."

For the first time, he noticed her skis leaning against the wall near the door with additional equipment. "I'll take these down while you say goodbye," he offered.

"All right. I'll meet you in the parking lot."

As he headed down the stairs with the skis, their bright red color made him smile. It would figure that she'd wear red on the slopes. Not one to be overlooked, was Sylvie. He'd been too distracted by the baby to tell her how pretty she looked in red. Remembering the red dress from their first date, he shook his head. Pretty was hardly the word to use. Mouthwatering, delectable, arousing…those words were more applicable.

Thinking of her clothing reminded him of yesterday, when he must have caught her just coming home after some type of exercise. She clearly hadn't been expecting anyone; the look on her face when she'd seen him at her door had been one of surprise.

He'd had to make a conscious effort to speak as well. Her hair had been caught up in a ponytail, and little silky wisps had escaped to slide around her ears and down her nape. She was wearing slim-fitting sweatpants that zipped up the sides and sturdy sneakers, but it was the brief sports bra top that had made his mouth go dry and scrambled his brain. It was *December,* for God's sake. What was she doing dressed in something that skimpy? But she hadn't appeared cold. Her arms were long and firmly muscled, and her skin held a dusky golden tone that he assumed was natural, since he doubted she'd been lying in the sun recently and he couldn't imagine Sylvie being vain enough—or standing still long enough—to go to a tanning parlor. Her bare torso was taut, without an ounce of extra flesh, though the firm mounds beneath the stretchy fabric of the bra told him that she wasn't that slender everywhere. She made his body react in an annoyingly adolescent way, and he'd had to force himself to shift his gaze to her face, not to grab her and devour her whole like he wanted to.

But her attitude had plainly told him he was there on sufferance only, and he'd known if he couldn't talk his way out of the mess he'd made he might never see her again outside the office. He didn't want to think about that, didn't want to acknowledge how badly he wanted to set things right between them. He was just finishing stowing her equipment when she came out of her apartment building toward him.

She was wearing her red ski coat over the black and red sweater she'd had on inside, and her eyes sparkled as she neared him. "Mission accomplished," she reported. "Let's head for the slopes!"

* * *

Sylvie was an avid skier and a natural athlete, nearly as good as he was. He suspected if she'd been skiing since she was four like he had, she'd have made him look bad. But he knew, because he asked her, that she'd only taken up the sport after starting work at Colette. Given her background, he imagined there hadn't been money for anything as expensive as skiing in her childhood.

They spent the entire evening on the mountain, conquering several of the trickier advanced slopes which had moguls to make things more interesting. The group, he'd discovered, was very loosely knit, with many members who'd only recently taken up the sport and who stuck near the beginner's slopes. Sylvie made an effort, though, to get around to every person who attended and say hello, dragging him with her for introductions.

His favorite part of the exercise, he decided, was the lift rides to the top of the mountain. He put his arm around her and listened as she chattered, but only half his attention was on her words. The enticing bow of her full red lips so near him was a pleasant kind of torture as he anticipated the next time he might get to set his mouth on hers. Her cheeks were flushed with color and her eyes snapped with excitement as she regaled him with stories of her first few times on the slopes.

Could there be a more beautiful woman in the world?

"I'm about ready to call it a night," she finally told him. Damn, but he wished she were saying that in a more intimate context!

They put away their equipment. Then he suggested they get a drink before they left, so they headed for the little bar above the pro shop. Walking up the stairs behind her, he had a perfect view of her curving figure in the slim-fitting ski pants and coordinating sweater. Her glossy dark hair bounced around her shoulders and he thought with amusement that it was just right for Sylvie, bouncy and vibrant and full of life.

They got cups of hot chocolate and settled at a tiny table in an alcove by the window. Marcus dragged his chair around to her side so that their backs were to the room and casually draped his arm around her shoulders. "I really enjoyed skiing with you," he told her. "We'll have to do it again."

"I try to go most Saturday evenings," she said. He was pleased to note that she didn't inch away or otherwise try to pretend that she didn't like his touch...which was a good thing, since he fully intended to touch every soft inch of glowing skin eventually.

"No dates?" He didn't even try to disguise the hungry intensity eating at him, letting his breath stir the fine strands dancing at her temples.

She shook her head and the curls cavorted more wildly. "Not often. I really haven't had a lot of time for men in my life."

He drew her closer. "And now?"

Her eyes danced but she didn't raise her head, only slanted him a coy glance from beneath her long, dark lashes. "And now...?"

"Now you have a man in your life." He lifted his hand, caressing her lips with his finger. He wanted badly to kiss her, but this wasn't the time or the place. The mere memory of the kisses they'd exchanged still had the power to rattle him and he was afraid he might lose what little common sense he appeared to have around her if he kissed her here.

A man's voice said, "Marcus? Marcus Grey?" and he

dropped his hand as the sensual daze in which he'd been floundering receded.

He rose automatically, turning to face a hefty, gray-haired man with a florid complexion. "Hello. I'm sorry—I don't believe—Solly! It's been years. How are you?"

"Good." The older man chuckled. "Saw you sit down. Wasn't sure it was you at first."

Marcus cleared his throat. "It's me. What are you doing here?" He grinned. "Taken up skiing?"

The older man gave a rolling laugh. "No way. I'm hanging out here waiting for my granddaughter and her friends to finish up their evening. Since I've retired, I've become the Sollinger family chauffeur."

Marcus chuckled. "Your family's well?"

"Both girls are married and have given us four grandchildren. The wife's retired, too."

"And keeping you busy, I bet." Both men laughed, and then Marcus remembered his manners and turned back to the table. "Sylvie, this is Earl Sollinger. Solly, Sylvie Bennett."

Sylvie rose and extended her hand. "It's nice to meet you, Mr. Sollinger."

"You too, little lady," boomed Solly. He looked expectantly from one of them to the other. "I didn't interrupt anything important, did I?"

"Of course not." Sylvie's face was flushed and she didn't look at Marcus. "Would you like to sit down?"

"No, no. I just wanted to say hello. It's been a long time." Solly's gaze met his, full of memories and old sorrows, and Marcus was abruptly catapulted back through the years of his childhood, years in which the solid foundation of his family had been tested and found flawed.

"It certainly has," he said quietly, his pleasure at the meeting fading. "Good seeing you, Solly."

"You, too," the older man said. "And say hello to your mother for me."

As Solly turned and wandered away, Marcus seated himself again, wrapping both hands around the paper cup of hot chocolate as if its warmth could dispel the chill that had invaded his heart.

"Marcus?" He turned his head. Sylvie was regarding him with a troubled expression on her face. "Are you all right?"

He nodded tightly. "Fine."

Then he jerked slightly as her soft hand settled on the back of his neck and rubbed at taut tendons and stretched nerves. "You don't seem fine. Did seeing Mr. Sollinger upset you?"

He shrugged. "No. Not really."

She fell silent. But the quiet between them wasn't a warm, companionable silence. The chatter of other patrons intruded and the lights behind them seemed bright and intrusive. Funny that he hadn't noticed that a moment ago. Out on the mountain, beneath the big floodlights, skiers looked like tiny doll figures gliding down the slopes.

Sylvie's hand was still on the back of his neck, gently massaging. "Do you want to go?" she asked, and it gave him an odd feeling. How had she known what he was thinking?

"Yes," he said, "if you're ready."

The drive back into Youngsville was quiet. But it wasn't entirely comfortable, Sylvie thought. Marcus had seemed preoccupied, distracted ever since that man, Mr. Sollinger, had stopped by their table. And it wasn't just preoccupation. He was unhappy. She could tell, even if he wouldn't admit it.

Maybe he couldn't even admit it to himself, she thought with a flash of insight. Maybe he needed someone to talk to, someone to bring him around to his feelings. Her breath caught in her throat. She wanted to be that someone. Was he willing to share that much of himself?

He made no secret of the fact that he wanted to sleep with her. She gulped as she remembered the passionate kisses they'd shared. But...he'd been all too willing to dismiss her from his mind when he'd gone away. Oh, he'd told her he'd thought of her, and she wanted to believe it. She guessed she *did* believe it, only...she'd been dismissed from thought before, discarded and never thought of again. And though she knew it was unfair to judge everyone she met by the standards of the lonely child she'd once been, a small kernel of doubt niggled at her mind.

She wasn't sure what Marcus intended this relationship to be, to lead to. She was pretty sure *he* didn't even know, if the grudging tone in which he'd admitted he couldn't stop thinking of her was anything to go by. She hid a small smile at the thought. So he couldn't get her out of his head, hmm?

That suited her just fine, because thoughts of him had begun to occupy every moment of her waking hours. She wanted to get to know him better. There'd never been a man before whom she couldn't dismiss, had never even been a man she particularly wanted to get to know, and until now all her considerable energies had been aimed at climbing her chosen career ladder. Her strategy had paid off, and she'd risen steadily through the ranks at Colette to her present position in Marketing.

But now, she wanted more. She wanted Marcus. The million-dollar question was: *What* did she want him for? She might not have much experience, but if she wanted hot, sizzling, scream-your-head-off sex, she was fairly certain he could deliver. The mere thought sent a tingle of wicked awareness pulsing through her body.

Okay, sex was a given. If this relationship went forward, that was going to be a part of it. But...deep in a part of her heart she was almost afraid to acknowledge, lurked another hopeful little thought, hesitantly waving its hand to get her attention. She wasn't even going to think about any words starting with *L,* she told herself sternly, because the chances of a man like Marcus Grey falling in lo—getting seriously heart-involved with someone like her, were next to none. Regardless of what Lila and Rose and her other friends thought about the silly coincidence of her wearing Rose's brooch the day they'd met.

Fidelity, though, and commitment for the duration of the time they were together, wasn't unreasonable, was it? Of course it wasn't. And it was time she stopped focusing so exclusively on her career and started thinking about the personal side of her life. This interlude with Marcus would be a good place to start. She wouldn't let it shatter her life when he left, as she knew he would, because she knew right up front he wasn't the kind of man for her— if, indeed, she needed a man in her life at all.

"You're awfully quiet," he observed. "What are you thinking?"

She jumped guiltily. "Ah, just wondering why you seem so blue all of a sudden."

There was a long silence in the car. She looked across at his profile, shadowed and occasionally outlined by the lights of streets and shops they passed as they came back into the city.

Finally, he sighed. "Solly was my father's best friend."

"Ah. And now you're thinking of your father." She was absurdly pleased that he'd confided in her. "I suppose if I'd ever known my parents I would miss them terribly when they passed away. I'm sorry."

"It isn't that." His jaw was tight. "Well it is—I mean, I do miss him, but—well, hell. I wish he could see what I've made of my life, you know?"

"You're certainly a financial success." Was that what he meant?

"Yeah. I am." He turned his head and glanced at her while they were waiting for a red light to change. "Do you know what happened to me today?"

"What?"

"I was approached by a person who shall remain nameless—because you'd recognize the name in an instant—about the possibility of joining their family through marriage."

She shook her head. "But who—? Oh my goodness," she said as realization struck. "You mean someone like a Rockefeller or a Hearst wanted you to marry their daughter?"

"Granddaughter," he corrected, not even cracking a smile.

She slumped in her seat. "Holy cow. I thought arranged marriages were a thing of the past."

He snorted. "Yeah. And Prince Charles would have married Diana Spencer if she'd been a barmaid."

"Point taken. But that's British royalty. We're Americans. Independent. Free. All that good stuff."

He didn't answer her.

"Okay," she said positively. "So you essentially got propositioned today. What does this have to do with your father?"

For the first time since they'd left the ski lodge, a wry smile touched his lips. "You certainly have a way of putting things in perspective, Sylvie." He turned off the engine and she was shocked to realize they were in the parking lot behind her building. She'd been so intent on him that she hadn't even noticed where they were. That was a little unnerving.

"Would you like to come up?" she asked. "I'd like to finish this conversation."

He looked at her through the darkness enshrouding the car and she shivered at the predatory tone in his voice. "I'd love to."

Five

She might have made a mistake, she thought nervously, inviting him to come up.

Sylvie carried two glasses of wine into her small living room, where Marcus already had made himself comfortable on the couch. "Here you go." She handed him a glass. "It's a California Pinot Noir that my boss gave me for my birthday. He knows about wine and says it's wonderful."

"And what do you say?" he asked idly, breathing deeply above the crystal glass that held the ruby liquid.

She shrugged and smiled. "I know roughly the same amount about wine that I do about babies."

His eyebrows rose. "Ah. Guess I won't be letting you peruse the wine list over dinner anytime soon."

She chuckled, swirling her wine and watching the patterns it made in the glass. "Don't worry. I know my strengths and weaknesses."

The words sounded more provocative than she'd intended, and she saw the dark gleam in his emerald eyes as he leaned closer. "Could I become one of your weaknesses, Sylvie?"

She couldn't look away; it was as if he physically held her gaze locked with his. She swallowed. "Possibly. Although I warn you, I'm not known for indulging myself."

His smile flashed, distinctly predatory, and she shivered at the intensity of his gaze. "That's all right. I like a challenge."

The words set off alarm bells in her head. "Marcus, I don't want to be considered a challenge." She straightened and stood, walking to the window. "Is that how you view your relationships with women? As challenges to be met and conquered?"

The silence behind her was absolute. She could almost feel the energy he was exerting to try to regroup and regain the ground he'd just lost. He rose, and she heard his muffled footfalls coming across the carpet until he stood directly behind her.

"I don't think of you as a challenge." His breath stirred the hair at the back of her neck and she shivered. "To me, you're a beautiful, desirable woman whom I'm enjoying getting to know. Whom I'd like to know even better." His hands settled on her shoulders, his thumbs gently rubbing along the sensitive sides of her neck. "Don't try to make it too complicated."

"But it *is* complicated," she said passionately, turning to face him. "You're going to shut the doors of a company I love."

"That's business," he said, sliding his big, warm hands down over her shoulders and arms until he settled them at her waist. "This isn't." Dropping his head, he sought her lips as he pulled her to him.

"It's all mixed up together," she said just before his lips closed over hers. He'd managed to evade a discussion of his feelings, she realized, but soon the thought was lost. The kiss that followed was a battle, a tender persuasion that undermined her stiff spine and her determination not to let him sidetrack her.

She couldn't resist him, was the last thought she had before she surrendered to the passion in his kiss, twining her arms around his neck and letting him press her back over his arm. As he deepened the kiss, sliding his tongue between her lips in an erotic dance of sensual foreplay, she moaned, opening her mouth more fully to his exploration, twisting in an effort to get closer to his lean hard body.

Complex feelings swirled through her. It could be far too easy to become addicted to this man, to wake up one morning and find that she *needed* him, that her day and her life would be incomplete without him.

The thought was shocking enough to shake her out of her pleasure and she began to struggle, withdrawing her arms from their stranglehold on his neck and shoving at his chest. She dragged her mouth from his, turning her head, but he merely shifted his focus, trailing his kisses along her jaw and down the sensitive flesh at the side of her neck. "Wait, Marcus."

She tore herself out of his arms and put a palm flat against his chest when he would have caught her to him again. "Wait," she repeated, aware that her breast was heaving as if she'd just run a five-minute mile.

He didn't look in much better shape, and after a long, tense moment when she wasn't sure he was going to let her go, he held both hands out, palm up, in surrender. "All right. I'm waiting. Now what?"

She took a deep breath. "Let's sit down."

Silently, he returned to the couch and waited until she was seated before sitting down beside her. Sylvie angled her body to face him. "Marcus," she said hesitantly, choosing her words carefully. "It's not that I don't like it when we…kiss. I do. Maybe too much. I told you before I'm not the kind of girl you want for a quick, easy…liaison. It's important to me that we get to know each other before we…before we…"

"Do the horizontal waltz?"

She sent him a reproving glance, but she couldn't prevent the snicker that slipped out. "Before we become physically intimate."

He sat forward and took her hands. "Sylvie, I want to make love to you. I've made no secret of it. But I don't want to pressure you. Tell me what you think you want. What you need from me."

"Time," she said simply. "I can't rush into this, no matter how badly I want to." She took a steadying breath and looked directly at him. "And I do want to," she said softly.

"Time." He flopped back against the couch, studying his watch. "An hour? A day?" But he was smiling.

"I'll know when it's time," she said. "You'll just have to trust me."

He stood. "Speaking of trust…I'd better get out of here while I can still be trusted." Taking her hand, he lifted her to her feet and tucked her against his side as he started for the door and his discarded outer layers. "What do you say to dinner tomorrow?"

She thought for a moment. "After six? I have some things to do in the afternoon."

"After six." He looked down at her intently, as if he were trying to read her mind. "And you can tell me what you did with your day."

"I will if you will," she said promptly.

"It's a deal." He took a deep breath and shrugged into his coat. "I'm not going to kiss you again because I don't trust myself to stop. I'll pick you up around six tomorrow."

She nodded. "Thank you for coming with me tonight."

A grin lifted the corners of his mouth. "Thank you for letting me invite myself."

It wasn't until he had gone that she realized that once again he'd managed to avoid sharing any real, meaningful information about himself with her.

She was still thinking about him the next morning as she changed out of her Sunday clothes and got into grubby old jeans after church. Her afternoon project was cookies. With a capital *C*.

Christmas was sneaking up on her this year. She'd been so caught up in worrying about the takeover attempt and the plans for the annual bachelorette auction she'd helped arrange to showcase Colette, Inc. jewelry and, ultimately, raise funds for a local orphanage, that she hadn't done a thing. Usually, by the time Thanksgiving arrived, her cards were signed, stamped and ready to go out the door on December first. This year…*yeesh*. She'd been working on them during her lunch hour, trying to get them finished before Christmas greetings became New Year's resolutions.

But today was cookie day. Every year she baked cookies to give to all her friends as gifts. Six or more different kinds. She'd made good old chocolate chip cookie dough months ago and frozen it, so now all she had to do was mix in the red-and-green holiday M&M's that she used in lieu of the chips and get it baking while she worked on other things. She greased cookie sheets while the oven preheated and then put four trays of cookies in to bake while she assembled the ingredients for peanut butter cookies, a quick and easy favorite. Her boss, Wil, begged her every year to include extra peanut butter cookies in his box.

After the peanut butter came big, soft sugar circles with chocolate drops pressed into their centers, and rice cereal-and-marshmallow treats colored with red and green food coloring that she made on the stove while the cookie baking continued. She had wanted to get the walnut-raisin cookies done today, too, but as she glanced at her watch she could see she wasn't going to get everything done before Marcus came to pick her up for their date tonight.

She was almost sorry she'd agreed to go out...but the way her breath backed up in her chest every time she thought of him would have made her a liar. At 5:30 p.m., she took the final batch of sugar cookies from the oven and set them out to cool. Long lines of cooling cookies marched all along her limited counter space and covered the top of her table. It was a good thing she didn't have a dog. Those cookies would make a tasty feast for a hungry pooch.

Someday, though, she thought as she dashed into her bedroom and tore off her clothes, then hopped into a quick shower. Someday she was going to have a dog. A big, tail-waving, tongue-lolling fool of a dog who would tolerate children climbing over him and lie under the table waiting for the food dropped during noisy family meals. The family wasn't something she could envision so clearly—and then a *very* clear picture leaped into her head: Marcus, with his big, competent hands cradling Jim's fussy baby yesterday afternoon.

A warm happiness flooded her thoughts. He'd looked so...so right. And she'd believed what he'd said about helping his secretary with her grandchildren because no man could be that comfortable with a baby unless he'd done it before. How many men in his position would be flexible enough—or approachable enough—to do that? Darn it, she'd been prepared to despise him, but from the very beginning he'd sneaked beneath her determination and tugged at her senses in far too many ways.

No, no, no! She shook her head so hard the barrette with which she'd clipped up her hair popped loose and her hair came tumbling down. She squealed and quickly turned off the shower before her hair could get really soaked. *See?* she told herself. *Marcus Grey is bad for you. Bad, bad, bad. You can enjoy him but you'd better not take him seriously.*

The trouble was, she thought as she pulled on panty hose and slipped into a burgundy silk coatdress, that she longed for someone to complete her little fantasy life. She wasn't stupid—she recognized that a part of her wanted a second chance, to recreate a more normal childhood through children of her own, to have children that would be loved and wanted. But Marcus couldn't possibly be that man. Could he?

Without warning, the amber brooch Rose had loaned her popped into her thoughts. Jayne, Lila and Meredith had all been wearing it when each of them had met the man of their dreams. Just as she'd worn it the day she'd met Marcus. Could there possibly be some magic—oh, that was ridiculous.

Of course there couldn't. It was simple coincidence. And in her case, it was simply that Marcus was the first man to whom she'd ever opened her heart. She'd protected herself for a long time and only now was she beginning to emerge from the cocoon of safety in which she'd encased her emotions. Marcus just happened to be in the right place at the right time. A man like him was so different from someone like her that there was no way they could ever connect in the middle. Not for a lifetime. She sighed, then shrugged. She couldn't change her past, but she was going to enjoy dating him while it lasted. She'd worry about a bruised heart later.

She dashed back into the bathroom and quickly made up her face, then turned on the blow-dryer and repaired the damage to her hair. And just in time—the doorbell rang as she was stepping into her pumps.

As she started for the door, the brooch caught her eye. Impulsively, she grabbed it and fastened it on one of her lapels. *Just because it looks so great with this dress,* she assured herself. Tomorrow she would *definitely* make time to return it to Rose.

When she opened the door, Marcus gave an appreciative whistle as she stepped back to invite him in while she got her coat.

He looked better every time she saw him. Tonight he was so clean-shaven she was sure he'd just used a razor before coming over, and his thick hair curled slightly where it had escaped the effects of his comb.

"Wow!" he said. "You look gorgeous—" He broke off, sniffing. "What's that smell?"

She sniffed blankly. "Smell?"

But he already was walking past her. "Cookies. I am in heaven," he declared. He didn't wait for an invitation but snagged a peanut butter cookie from the corner of the counter and bit into it. "Mmm." He reached for her with his free hand, pulling her against his side before she could protest and grinning at her. "It's delicious. Want a bite?"

"No, and if you eat any more, I won't give you any for Christmas," she told him. Her heart was beating too fast and it was hard to breathe. She'd been ready to say hello, not to be dragged to him like a doll. Her body was pressed against him from neck to knee. In fact, his leg was practically between hers and as she began to struggle to move away, the laser intensity of his green eyes turned to her once more.

"Hello," he murmured. He raised a hand and cradled one side of her face and she stilled. "I missed you."

She was stunned, both by the unexpectedly tender gesture and his words. He'd missed her? "You just saw me last night." She tried to keep her voice casual.

"I know." A small vertical line appeared between the thick slashes of his eyebrows and it deepened as she watched. He released her and turned away, and she got the distinct impression that his mood had changed in that instant. "Are you ready?" he asked. His tone was still courteous and friendly but the deeply intimate warmth it had held was gone, and abruptly she was sure of it.

She raised her chin. "Yes, if you're sure you still want to take me out."

He picked up the coat that she'd draped over the chair nearest the door. "Of course I still want to take you out," he said. He smiled at her. If she didn't know better, she'd think she'd imagined his withdrawal. But there was something watchful in the depths of his gaze and she realized she hadn't imagined anything.

"Wait," she said. "I have to put these cookies away."

"I'll help."

She laughed, determined not to let his weird moods bother her. "I'll just bet. You stay right over there—" she pointed to her high-ceilinged living room, "and I'll take care of these.'' In a few minutes, she had all her handiwork packed away in tins.

Walking to him, she let him help her don her coat before preceding him out the door. He was charming and pleasant as he put her into his car and drove to Crystal's, a French restaurant at which he'd reserved a table in a small alcove by a fireplace. There was no way to approach the topic of his abrupt mood change, short of simply asking him what had been wrong, and she was beginning to recognize his evasive maneuvers by now. When he didn't want to discuss something, Marcus could be an incredibly sneaky devil.

''So I guess I know what you did today,'' he said after they'd settled back with a bottle of red burgundy that he'd approved. ''My question is, why would a young, single woman make that many cookies?''

''Would you believe I only bake once a year and freeze them all?''

A snort of sarcastic amusement was his only response.

''I bake every year,'' she told him. ''That's what I give many of my friends for Christmas. I bake six or seven different kinds of cookies and package them in assortments of one and two dozen.''

He whistled. ''Pretty labor-intensive, isn't it?''

''No more so than the endless shopping most people do,'' she replied. ''I enjoy this and my friends all seem to appreciate my efforts. And this way, my shopping is very manageable.''

''Am I going to get cookies this year?'' he asked with a sly smile.

She shrugged carelessly. ''I hadn't really thought about it.'' And pigs flew. What to get Marcus for Christmas had been on her mind as she'd worked all day. Should she get him anything? Was that presuming too much?

Should she just give him cookies like she gave her many friends? The man was immensely wealthy. She couldn't give him anything that he couldn't buy for himself, probably better and more expensive.

"Sylvie," he said, leaning forward, and his manner was intense enough to make her sit up and pay attention. "I want cookies. I *need* cookies. In fact, you could just let me buy the entire kitchen full from you."

She burst out laughing. "Then what would I give my friends for Christmas?"

He spread his hands. "You could do more shopping."

The waiter came and took their orders and after he went away again, she asked, "So you know what I did today. How about you?"

"Wheeling and dealing," he said dismissively. "That's pretty much what I do every day."

"So specifically what were you working on today?" She desperately wanted to get to know the man beneath the charming mask and it frustrated her immensely that he seemed to sidestep her every effort.

He hesitated, as if he were warring with himself. Then he said, "Today I toured a plant in Ohio that manufactures steel. I've been looking for the perfect opportunity for several years because another one of my industries uses large quantities of steel and it would be far cheaper to manufacture it ourselves. I'm hoping to buy out this company."

"Any disgruntled stockholders?"

"Very funny." He sent her a mock-glare. "They have all the equipment we need but more important, they have a unique method for bending sheet steel that I'd like to have. It's a closely guarded secret and until I buy the company, they won't divulge their process."

She raised her eyebrows. "Smart."

He nodded. "From their perspective. From mine, it's annoying as hell. I'd really like to be in production with the new system by March first but the longer we dicker over details, the less chance I have of getting things up and running by then."

She could see he was dead serious. He had the same look on his face he'd worn in that meeting she'd disrupted the day they'd met. Intense, competitive, focused. She pitied any business that got in his way when Marcus got that gleam in his eye. Look at what was happening to Colette.

Thinking about her own employer made her realize that she didn't have any idea what his plans for her company were now.

"You're going to ask me about Colette," he said.

She was surprised. "Am I that transparent?"

He considered. "No, but I guess I'm beginning to learn how your mind works."

There was a brief silence between them. She waited but he didn't speak again.

"Are you going to tell me?"

"Am I going to tell you what?" he countered.

She could feel irritation rising. If he was trying to annoy her, he was doing a pretty good job of it. Just as she opened her mouth, a feminine voice said, "Marcus! I didn't know you were dining here tonight."

Sylvie looked up. A petite silver-haired woman stood by their table with a tall, slender, impeccably dressed man lightly holding her elbow. Marcus stood, drawing the woman to him and kissing her cheek. "Mother. I didn't expect you, either." He extended a hand to the man. "Good to see you, Drew."

Then he turned to Sylvie. "Mother, I'd like to introduce Ms. Sylvie Bennett. Sylvie, this is my mother Isadora Cobham Grey, and her escort, Drew Rice."

Too shaken to do more than smile, Sylvie extended her hand to each of the older people. His mother!

"Hello, Sylvie." Drew was the first one to break the silence. "It's a pleasure to meet you." Marcus's mother's…whatever he was—boyfriend?—had warm blue eyes.

"Thank you." She finally found her voice. "You, also, and you, Mrs. Grey."

"It's just Izzie, dear," said Mrs. Grey. "I've never been a very formal person, have I, Marcus?" She smiled fondly at her son.

"No." He smiled back and a sudden, ridiculous stab of envy shot through Sylvie. The love between them was evident, as was their shared blood. Marcus had gotten his green eyes from his mother, as well as a certain shape to his face through the temples and cheekbones. As a little girl, she'd always wondered if there was anyone else out there in the world who looked like her. She still caught herself sometimes, staring at strangers' faces, wondering if one of them could be the woman who'd walked away from her child.

"Are you from Youngsville, Sylvie?" asked his mother.

"Yes, ma'am. I've lived here all my life."

"I don't believe I know any Bennetts." Izzie Grey's eyes were kind; the comment hadn't been a dig.

"I'm an orphan," she said quietly. "I spent my early years at St. Catherine's. I got a scholarship to the University of Michigan and after I graduated, I came back here. I work at Colette," she added. She couldn't resist glancing at Marcus. "The firm your son is trying to buy and liquidate."

Marcus shot her a warning frown. "Sylvie—"

"What?" His mother's voice sounded distressed and Sylvie was sorry she'd spoken without considering her words. "Marcus, why would you want Colette?"

"It's just a good business decision," he said defensively. "It has nothing to do with…anything, Mother."

"We just returned yesterday from six months in Europe," Drew said to Sylvie. Hmm, a definite boyfriend. "I looked through some of the back issues of the paper this morning and read about Marcus's plans there."

"And you didn't tell me?" Isadora turned to him with a wounded expression.

Drew shrugged, putting his arm around her shoulders and drawing her protectively against his side. "I forgot."

"That old emerald fiasco cost Frank his company," said Marcus's mother heatedly. "How could you forget to tell me anything that involved Colette?"

"Emerald fiasco?" Marcus's voice was sharp. "What are you talking about?"

Mrs. Grey searched her son's face for a long moment. Sylvie saw comprehension dawn just as the older woman whispered, "He never told you, did he?"

"Told me what?" Marcus appeared unaware that three of the four of them were standing, but Drew pulled out a chair and gently ushered Isadora into it, then took the remaining one for himself. Marcus reluctantly took his own seat again. "Colette lured away Dad's top design team and shortly afterward, Van Arl went bankrupt. I've never heard anything about any emeralds."

"Before the employees started leaving," said his mother, "there was a…a problem. Carl Colette accused your father of selling him fake emeralds. Of course, your father never would have done such a thing, so he quietly set up a plan to expose the real culprit. Eventually, he

caught his chief buyer attempting a second, similar trans-
action, but by then rumors about Van Arl's integrity already had affected sales. He had to start letting people
go. It wasn't until then that the design team went to Colette."

There was a short silence at the table.

Finally, Marcus stirred. "Well, thank you for telling
me, but it makes no difference to my plans. My business
acquires companies and this is simply another profitable
opportunity."

Drew Rice took command of the conversation before
Isadora could argue with Marcus, though it was clear she
wasn't happy as they said their goodbyes and left to find
their own table.

On their heels came the waiter with their dinners. Marcus was extremely quiet while they ate. She couldn't even
imagine what he must be thinking. Why hadn't his father
ever told him the whole story? Marcus had grown up
believing that Carl Colette's company was entirely responsible for his father's failure.

After spending a solid ten minutes silently debating
with herself whether or not she should bring up the topic,
she said, "Your mother doesn't seem to blame Carl Colette for Van Arl's demise."

He acted, for one endless moment, as if he hadn't
heard her. He chewed the bite in his mouth thoroughly,
swallowed, set down his fork and took a sip of wine
before his gaze finally met hers. "You don't understand," he said, and his hand on the tabletop was a fist.

"Then explain it to me," she said, reaching out and
covering his hand with hers. "Help me to see it as you
do."

His emerald eyes bored into hers. Beneath her hand,
muscles flexed and she could see another one working in

his jaw. Finally, he said, "What do you know about my parents' backgrounds?"

She shook her head, perplexed by the question. "Ah, your mother is one of the Chicago Cobhams. Old, prestigious family with ties to Great Lakes shipping. Your great-grandfather was a friend of Teddy Roosevelt's, your grandfather is rumored to have been intimately involved in keeping a lid on Kennedy's affair with Marilyn Monroe because of his friendship with the Bouvier family. Your father had Van Arl." She thought for a moment. "I don't think I know anything else about him."

"I'd be very surprised if you did," he said evenly, the words clipped off as if he didn't want to let them escape. "My father was the son of a sailor who died in a storm on Lake Michigan two months before Dad was born. My grandmother quickly grew too poor to feed five children so they were sent to foster homes."

Sylvie winced. She hadn't realized this would hit so close to home.

"My father did well in school and he graduated from high school, although he got his diploma two years late because he'd had to quit school to work several times. He got a scholarship to college and that's where he met my mother."

He stopped for another sip of wine and she did the same, shaken by the story. She'd assumed his father also came from a moneyed family.

"My mother's family wasn't enthusiastic about their marriage but Dad and Mom were in love and determined. After the wedding, Dad risked everything he owned to purchase Van Arl. I was born a year later." He paused, and his eyes were hot when he looked at her. "You already dug up the rest of the story, but what you don't know is what it did to my father. He *needed* to succeed in her world. The failure of Van Arl broke him. My father believed he had failed my mother—and her family didn't make it any easier. He was completely humiliated. It…changed him. He withdrew from her, from everyone. When I was seven my parents divorced.'' He glanced away. ''My mother loved him until the day he died, but he couldn't let himself accept it. Just a few years ago, she renewed her childhood friendship with Drew, although she swears she'll never marry again.''

''Drew seems like a nice man,'' she murmured, not knowing what else to say. The sad story of his childhood made her wonder what he'd seen and heard during those fragile, formative years. No wonder he was so determined to build his own empire. He wasn't about to let anyone take anything away from him. Not just anything as tangible as a fortune, but the intangibles like love and security. If he didn't allow himself to need them, he couldn't be hurt by the lack of them, either.

''Drew is a nice man,'' he said, but there was a note of cynicism in his voice. ''And what's even better, he's from Mother's world. Money, social distinction, generations of distinguished ancestors. Nothing for the Cobhams to object to.'' His voice was bitter.

She groped for words. She'd seen him determined, she'd seen him charming. Scrupulously polite, ridiculously silly, completely annoying. But she'd never seen him look defeated before.

Quietly, she said, ''I do understand, now, why you feel the way you do about Colette. But after what your mother just told us, you must realize Colette bears no responsibility for what happened to your father.''

Unexpectedly, Marcus slapped both hands down on the table, making the dishes rattle. Sylvie jumped and instinctively drew back. ''You're like a damned broken record,'' he said, and there was a shocking, vicious fury in his tone. ''All you think about is that precious company. I don't get it. You don't own it. You aren't even an executive. But your life would be empty if they fired you tomorrow.''

She sucked in a single shocked breath as the ugly words hung between them. As if from a great distance, she heard herself say, ''Thank you for your opinion, Mr. Grey.'' Shoving back her chair, she grabbed her purse and rapidly walked out of the dining room.

''Sylvie! Get back here.'' She heard his commanding voice behind her.

''Not a chance in hell,'' she muttered, breaking her own rule about swearing for the first time in years. Reaching the front lobby, she realized her coat was checked and Marcus held the claim ticket. Okay, she'd suffer without the coat. She'd survive. Because there was no way she *ever* intended to speak to Mr. Marcus Grey again.

Bursting through the glass doors without breaking pace, she started for the corner where she knew she could catch a taxi. It was freezing outside, a brisk wind from the lake blowing right in her face, but she wasn't about to go back inside.

''Sylvie, wait!'' Marcus pushed through the doors. ''You don't even have your coat. I'm sorry for what I said—''

''Stay away from me,'' she shouted over her shoulder. ''I do not need you in my life.'' Picking up her stride, she hurried forward before he could catch up. Then the world tilted sideways and she lurched as her high-heeled pumps skidded across a patch of ice. She knew she was falling but before she could do more than throw out a hand, her head banged solidly into the sidewalk.

There was one searing burst of pain and then... nothing.

Six

"**S**ylvie!" More panicked than he'd ever been in his life, Marcus sprinted to where she had fallen on the slippery sidewalk. As he realized she wasn't moving, wasn't making any effort to rise or even sit up, sheer terror screamed through him. "Call 9-1-1!" he shouted over his shoulder to a group of pedestrians who had turned when he'd run past.

He fell to his knees beside Sylvie, ripping off his jacket and throwing it over her.

What had possessed her to run off without her coat?

Guilt stabbed viciously. He knew exactly what had possessed her. A better question was: what the hell had possessed him, that he had lashed out at her that way? He prided himself on never losing control. His employees and competitors called him Nerves of Steel, because he never, ever allowed himself to show anger or frustration, not even when a really sweet deal fell through.

He pressed his fingers to her pulse even as he noted that her chest was rising and falling in the rhythms of breathing. Though he knew she shouldn't have died from a mere fall, relief still nearly felled him completely. He bent over her to look at her face and the side of her head where she lay against the pavement, and fear again took over as he saw a spreading dark stain in the dim light. He put his fingers to it, knowing the moment he touched the warm, viscous fluid that it was Sylvie's blood.

He bowed his head, fighting the instinct to gather her into his arms and carry her to a warm, safe place. He couldn't move her.

It seemed like hours before the ambulance came tearing down the street. He leaped to his feet and waved his arms. "She's over here." He told them, in succinct tones, that she had fallen. No, she hadn't been moved. No, she hadn't made any movements or spoken. No, she hadn't shown any signs of consciousness since then.

As the EMTs eased her onto a body board, he realized his hands were shaking. Someone put his jacket over his shoulders. One medic said, "Are you her husband?"

He shook his head. "No, but I'm—" He stopped. *I'm what? The guy who made her fall? The guy who knows he'll never be the same if anything happens to her?*

The medic put a friendly hand on his shoulder. "We're taking her to Mercy. Can you get there?"

He nodded, pulling himself together and yanking on his suit coat as his brain began to function again. Keys. Claim check for her coat. Valet parking ticket. That was important. As his car was pulled around, he felt a hand touch his elbow. He turned and looked into his mother's face. Drew was right behind her.

"Sylvie slipped on the ice," he said. "I have to go—"

"We heard," Isadora Grey said. "Do you want us to come with you?"

"No." He felt too guilty and afraid to want anyone to see him right now. "But I'll call you as soon as I hear anything," he offered.

His mother nodded. "I'll say a prayer for her."

"Thank you." He rushed around to the driver's side and thrust a bill into the hand of the waiting attendant. He was out of the parking lot before the valet had pocketed his tip.

Mercy was the closest hospital and, as it turned out, the one he would have wanted her taken to if he'd been given a choice. Private, well-staffed, a solid reputation. In the E.R., he barely had Sylvie's name out of his mouth before the receptionist said, "She's being X-rayed. Have a seat and the doctor will be out to speak with you as soon as he can."

"Thank you." He sank into an uncomfortable vinyl chair, reliving over and over again the sickening moment when he'd seen Sylvie go down and known he was too far away to catch her. He thought of how still and silent she'd been. God, she'd looked so small on that gurney. She *was* small, he recalled with a pang. She was so feisty and amusing that he tended to forget how fragile her slender limbs were, how small her hands felt nestled in his, the way his chin fit against her temple when he held her. His throat grew tight and he ducked his head as he slouched in the chair.

Nearly an hour later, a short man in blue scrubs with a mask hanging around his neck pushed through the doors. Marcus shot to his feet. "How's Sylvie?"

The man held out a hand. "I'm Dr. Calter. Are you Ms. Bennett's next of kin?"

"She has none," Marcus said, returning the handshake. "But I'm close enough." Perhaps not strictly true, but he intended to see Sylvie and that seemed the most expedient way. "How is she?"

"She regained consciousness in the ambulance and appears to be coherent. She has seven stitches in the contusion along her hairline. There is no obvious internal damage, no evidence of skull fracture or concussion." The doctor raised his eyebrows. "She will, of course, need to be watched carefully. If there are any changes, bring her back in immediately."

Marcus waited.

The doctor looked at him. "Any questions?"

"That's it? She doesn't have any other injuries?"

The man smiled. "Not that we were able to discern."

"May I see her?"

"She's still being treated but she should be done shortly. I'll have the nurse call you when she's ready to go." He didn't like it but he knew Sylvie wouldn't be happy if he made a scene. Remembering his mother's request, he called her and assured her that Sylvie was all right. Then, as he replaced the receiver, he remembered Sylvie's friendship with Rose Carson. Sylvie wouldn't want Rose to worry when she didn't come home, he was sure. Just as he hung up the phone from the second call, the receptionist called, "Sylvie Bennett's family?"

He followed the nurse through the E.R. In the hallway just outside the door of the cubicle in which she rested, he paused and took a deep breath. What was he going to say to her? An apology wasn't adequate. Slowly, he exhaled and pushed the door open. Even if she hated his guts from now on, he had to see her, had to know she was all right.

It was dark in the room and he realized with a jolt that it was nearly midnight. One small light, with its beams facing the ceiling, cast a cool white glow around the head of the bed. He walked to her side. "Sylvie?" he said in a hushed voice.

Her eyes had been closed and he saw the effort it took for her to raise her lids. He knew the moment she realized who was beside her bed. Her withdrawal was total, a pulling back of her whole self as she turned her face to the wall. "Go away."

His throat felt odd, tight. "I can't."

She didn't respond.

"I'm sorry for what I said." He hesitated, then faced an ugly truth. "I was hurting and I took it out on you."

Still no response.

"You don't have to forgive me," he said. "I probably don't deserve it. But you need to know that no other woman has ever made me feel the way you do. No other woman has ever made me take a closer look at myself and address my flaws." He hesitated again. "Is there anyone you want me to call?"

Still no response. His throat grew even tighter and he swallowed. "You're being discharged now. I'm taking you home."

Again, she didn't react. Then, just as he was beginning to think he'd blown it forever, she moved. Though her head still faced the wall, the arm closest to him slowly slid across the coverlet in his direction. He swallowed again, cursing the tightness in his chest he couldn't seem to get rid of. Then he reached out and gently folded his fingers around her much smaller ones, closing his own eyes on a wave of shaky relief when her hand curled into his.

She woke early and for a long moment, had no idea where she was. And just as she had when she was a child trying desperately to fit into whatever home she'd been placed in at the time, she lay perfectly still, assessing everything with her senses before moving a muscle. A dull ache throbbed in her head. Nothing else seemed to be damaged, she decided, as she slowly, carefully tested each limb.

Once she'd ascertained her physical status, she looked around. The room was a restful light cream color with a pattern of ivy leaves crawling over the wallpaper on one wall. Two large windows sported matching curtains and the covers on her bed also echoed the ivy motif. A pretty ormolu clock, ticking on the small table beside the bed, read 6:02 a.m.

The bed. A door opened in her mind and she had a vague memory of Marcus carrying her in here last night. She realized, with a start of shock, that he must have brought her to his home. At the same instant, she realized her right hand was firmly held in someone else's. Turning her head slightly, she saw that Marcus sat in a chair pulled close to the side of the bed. He was bent forward at the waist, one arm on the bed with his head cradled on it. His other hand was holding hers.

Had he been there all night? She studied his face, the dark slash of his eyebrows, the black crescents of lashes shielding those piercing green eyes, his mouth a firm line even in sleep.

No other woman has ever made me feel the way you do. His voice was clear in her head and slowly the memory of the night before came swimming into her fuzzy brain. He'd been furious with her. She knew why, because she was coming to understand him.

As a child, his parents' divorce must have devastated him. She winced, feeling a flood of sympathy for the little boy as she remembered what a vulnerable age he'd been.

And now to learn that his father hadn't been completely straight with him, that perhaps he, Marcus, was pursuing a goal for the wrong reasons... He'd built a world for himself in which he was always in control, in which no one could hurt him. He might not be able to admit to a conscious goal of dismantling Colette, but she was sure that in some deep corner of his psyche, that little boy would cheer the day that the company he believed destroyed his father ceased to exist.

And when she'd forced him to confront the possibility that he was wrong, he'd lashed out. She sighed, turning her face toward the windows. Why had he brought her here? In the short time they'd known each other, they'd had more disagreements and misunderstandings than she had in all the relationships she'd ever had lumped together. Why wouldn't he give up?

At the thought of him walking out the door, of never seeing him again, never feeling his arms strong and secure around her, his lips arousing and enticing on hers, her heart squeezed painfully.

She was in love with him.

Finally, she saw the truth she'd been avoiding. She loved the intensity with which he pursued his goals, the quick humor and intelligence he displayed in their battles of wits. She loved the way his broad shoulders tapered to lean, fit hips and thighs, the way his eyes darkened with desire when he wanted her. She loved the way he seemed to know what she was thinking before she said it—she'd never been that close to another person in her life. It was a little scary to realize that he'd come to know her so well so easily, but she took consolation from the thought that she'd come to know him nearly as well, despite their differing viewpoints on the matter of Colette.

Colette. She recognized that her attachment to the company was no more reasonable or rational than his desire to expunge it was. And if he succeeded, she had little doubt that he would take care of the employees, even though the rumor mill had cooked up all sorts of horrid stories.

When she'd been digging into his past, she discovered that though he was known for trimming dead wood and salary overhead from the companies he acquired, he also was decent and generous to those he let go, providing continued benefits and a good severance package as well as references. He didn't come in and slash blindly, but had a team of experts assess the company from every angle before taking any steps. He was honorable in a way that fit the code by which he'd lived his life.

But still, the bottom line was that he wanted to shut the doors of the company that had given her her first job and nurtured her in countless ways.

Glancing back at him, she was unnerved to see his eyes open, watching her. Though she was far from ready to face a reckoning, she had little choice. She squared her shoulders.

"Good morning," Marcus said.

She smiled. "Morning, yes. The good part is debatable." She hesitated, then figured she might as well just get it over with. "I'm sorry I behaved so foolishly last night. I regret inconveniencing you like this."

He regarded her steadily. "Who said I was inconvenienced?"

She didn't have an answer to that.

"Worried sick might be a better way to put it." The green flame of his gaze disappeared as his eyes closed for a moment. "I felt so helpless when I saw you fall. I couldn't get to you in time."

There was an anguish in his tone that surprised her. She slid her hand from his and laid it along the side of his face. "Marcus, it wasn't your fault."

He lifted a hand and covered hers with it, then turned his head and pressed a kiss into her palm. "I know. But knowing I was the reason you rushed out in the first place doesn't make me feel very good." He scowled. "I should have stopped you."

She couldn't prevent herself from caressing his cheek with her fingertips. "How? I wasn't about to listen to reason. If that ice hadn't been there, I'd have been gone before you could catch me."

"Neither of us was particularly reasonable." He took her hand from his face and brushed his lips over her fingers, then folded her smaller hand in his. "What's important right now is that you rest and get well."

"I'm in your home?"

He nodded. "I thought it would be best to keep you here at my house for a few days, until you're feeling better."

"What?" She couldn't sit up but she turned her head on the pillow to get a better view of him. "I can't stay here."

"You can't take care of yourself," he argued. "And you're not supposed to be moving around a lot for at least twenty-four hours. You go back to the doctor on Wednesday. Until then, you can't be by yourself."

"I need to get home," she said. "I'll be fine." No way was she going to live with him. Not for an hour, not for a day. It would be entirely too easy to get dependent on him for her happiness. She'd been perfectly happy alone for the past twenty-seven years and she refused to allow that to change just because she'd been dumb enough to fall for a completely unsuitable man. "You seem to forget that I've lived alone for a long time."

"I don't care," he said. "You're not staying there alone." He stood and stretched, ignoring the killing look she aimed at him. "I'll be back with your breakfast in a little bit. Don't get up without me."

It made her feel marginally better to stick out her tongue at his broad back as he left the room.

In thirty minutes he was back. He'd taken the time to shave and shower, and he carried a breakfast tray.

Setting the tray on a dresser, he moved forward and put his arm around her, ignoring her efforts to shoo him away. "Let me help," he said, bending his head down to hers. "Stop fighting me, Sylvie."

She wanted to argue more, she really did, but the mere act of sitting up had made her amazingly dizzy. She was shaken to realize that all she appeared to be wearing were her undergarments and a man's dress shirt.

"Where are my clothes?" she asked, very aware of the flimsy covering. "And why am I wearing this?"

Marcus cleared his throat. "It was the only thing I could think of that I wouldn't have to slip over your head. Fortunately, I had an extra shirt in the car or you might have left the hospital wearing one of their gowns."

She stared at him, slowing realizing that her dress had probably been ruined, if not by the fall, then by the blood she'd undoubtedly shed. "Great," she said ruefully. "I never thought about that."

"Later, I'll bring you some of your own things," he offered.

"Later, you can take me home," she said firmly.

He didn't respond and she chose to take that as acceptance. Turning to the dresser, he brought the tray over and set it across her lap.

"Did you do this?" she asked suspiciously.

He shook his head. "I have a housekeeper. She got it ready." He efficiently uncovered the food, buttered and cut up her pancakes, poured syrup over them, cut up her bacon and added cream to her coffee—and she was exhausted just from watching him. Okay, so she might have a little trouble preparing meals. She'd manage, she thought, as he lifted a forkful of pancakes to her mouth.

"My mother called," he said when she stopped to take a sip of orange juice. "She was very concerned about you."

"You told your mother?" She was horrified. Isadora Grey was the very picture of ladylike decorum. What must she think of a girl who would have a public spat with her son?

"I didn't have to tell her," he said. "They were there when the ambulance took you away."

She closed her eyes. "Good grief. What must she think of me?"

He looked puzzled. "She was going home to say a prayer for you last night. I imagine that's mostly what she was thinking."

"No," she said, twisting her fingers as she tried to explain. "Your mother is such a…a lady. Good breeding oozes out of her pores. She probably thinks I'm terrible, fighting with you like that."

He chuckled. "Quit worrying. I don't think she knows about our, ah, disagreement. She only heard that you fell."

"Oh." She was ridiculously relieved. "Thank heavens."

"For what it's worth," he told her, "she liked you. She said you didn't seem like the type to let me get away with anything."

That made her smile. "We barely spoke. How could she have come to that conclusion?"

He snorted. "It probably wasn't your meek and mild attitude."

She narrowed her eyes. "Watch it, buddy." They smiled at each other, pleased with the repartee. Finally, she said, "I appreciate everything you've done for me, Marcus, but I meant it when I said I couldn't stay here. Rose always worries if we're late. She's probably beside herself if she's realized I never came home last night."

"I called her."

She stopped. Stared. "You called her?"

To her surprise, a dull red color crept into his cheeks. "Well, yeah. I thought she might worry about you. She was, uh, going to call somebody named Meredith." Abruptly, he stood and headed for the door.

"Marcus." He stopped. "That was nice of you. Thank you."

Slowly, he turned to face her, his expression sober. "You're welcome." But her attention was distracted from him as the door behind him slowly opened. It was eerie, as if an unseen hand were guiding it.

He must have seen the alarm in her eyes because he turned quickly. Then she heard him let out a breath of laughter. "All right, you big snoop. Come on in and meet the lady."

Who on earth was he talking to? Sylvie watched, astounded as a fluffy white cat regally stalked into the room, tail waving like a large plume, and wound around Marcus's legs. A cat… She'd never had a pet of any kind. Her only experience with cats was with her friend Jayne's sister's pet, Jujube, who had declared war the day he came for an extended visit while Jayne's sister attended college. Dealing with that monster was enough to put a person off cats forever. Same for the candy by the same name.

She'd never have suspected Marcus of being a cat fan. Weren't big masculine he-men supposed to like big, tough dogs? As she watched her big masculine he-man bend and scoop the feline gently into his arms, cradling it like a baby, she realized this was a whole new side to a man she thought she'd had pegged as an aggressive corporate shark.

Or maybe it wasn't. She could recall with perfect clarity how he'd looked holding Jim's baby girl. She'd nearly melted on the spot as she'd watched him that day. *Not,* she assured herself, because she was entertaining any thoughts of him as fatherhood material!

It was nearly noon by the time he pulled into the parking lot behind 20 Amber Court with Sylvie in the seat beside him. He'd left her resting, with the cat lying beside her purring like an outboard motor, while he got on the phone and ordered pajamas and a robe from a local boutique for her to wear home. The store had been short-handed so he'd offered to drive down and pick up the clothes. And he'd extracted a promise from her that she wouldn't get out of bed until he got back.

He grinned, thinking of how grumpy and reluctant she'd been to make that promise. Until he'd heard the words from her lips, he wasn't leaving, because he knew exactly how strong-willed and independent she could be. As it was, he'd been anxious about leaving her for too long, in case she came up with some plausible reason why she'd had to break her promise.

Now he came around and opened the car door, leaning in to lift her out.

"Really, Marcus. I can walk."

She'd said the same thing when he'd carried her from the guest bed to the car, and his response was the same as well. "Maybe, but you're not going to." As he entered the building and crossed to the foot of the imposing marble staircase, a door opened and Rose Carson peeked out.

When she saw them, she quickly yanked open the door and stepped into the hallway. "Oh, Sylvie, how are you feeling? I've been so upset since Marcus called me last night!"

"Sylvie's all right, Mrs. Carson." He stopped. "Well, no she's not, but I'm taking care of her."

"Yes, and little Sylvie can speak for herself," she said testily. She had one arm around his neck and he winced as she tugged—hard—on a lock of his hair.

Rose smiled. "That's my Sylvie. I guess you weren't hurt too badly." She turned to Marcus, pointing to a discreetly placed elevator near the back of the hallway that he hadn't noticed before. "Let's take the elevator."

As they rode up, Rose said, "So tell me exactly how it happened."

He felt Sylvie tense slightly in his arms. "We went to dinner," she said quietly. "I slipped on some ice coming out of the restaurant and knocked myself out." He glanced down at her. Their eyes met, and she looked away. It wasn't exactly a lie…but she'd definitely omitted some things. She was a very private person, for all her genuine kindness to others. He could imagine that she wouldn't want the world to know that they'd been arguing.

"Thank goodness you weren't hurt worse," Rose said. "I swear, every winter someone in my bridge club falls and breaks an arm or a hip. That ice is treacherous."

He followed as the landlady—whom he knew was far more than simply a widow with an apartment building—

bustled through the apartment into a soft, welcoming bedroom. Although it was done in white like the living area, the accents in here were a soft lilac and green, and he waited until Rose pulled back the quilt and sheets before laying Sylvie down on the bed. "I'll let Marcus help you get settled," Rose said to Sylvie, "but if you need anything, you just call down to me. I'll be up with some soup later. And I'll let Jayne, Lila and Meredith know you're home. I'm sure they will want to stop by and see that you're truly all right."

Sylvie reached out a hand and drew Rose close, hugging her. "Thank you," she said. "I appreciate…I mean, thank you for…" She trailed off and Marcus was surprised to see tears glistening in her dark eyes. "I'm sorry if you were worried."

As the older woman's arms closed about Sylvie, he realized that this was far more than just a neighborly relationship. Knowing how long she'd known Rose, he suspected that the landlady was almost a surrogate mother to Sylvie…but he wondered if Sylvie understood how much Rose cared for her.

As Rose straightened and walked from the room, he followed her. "Could I have a moment, Rose?"

In answer, she beckoned him to the door, then closed it quietly behind them when he stepped into the hall with her.

"Sylvie doesn't know that you own Colette stock, does she?"

Rose shook her head. "No."

"How much do you own?"

She took a deep breath. "The forty-eight percent you weren't able to buy."

"Whoa." He knew his face betrayed his shock. He'd assumed she owned a few shares. "I thought members of the Colette family owned that stock. How did you get it?''

Rose regarded him steadily. "Promise me that what I'm going to tell you will remain in confidence. I'm not ready to tell anyone else."

He nodded. "All right."

She clasped her hands together, as if she were a child getting ready to recite. "Carl Colette was my father. My full name is Teresa Rose Colette Carson. There are no other members of the family."

"Ah—" He started to speak, but Rose cut him off.

"Marcus—Mr. Grey, I know how you must feel about Colette after the way your father lost his business. But please, if it's revenge you want, punish me. Change the company name if you like, but don't make all those loyal employees pay for a sad misunderstanding that happened more than a quarter-century ago."

Great. Here was yet another person who believed the worst of him, who apparently had taken the ugly rumors as gospel truth. "Mrs. Carson, I assure you I have no intention of making the current employees pay." Then something she'd said caught his attention. "You wouldn't care if I changed the company name? It's your family heritage, after all."

"My heritage." Her tone was bitter and her still-pretty face suddenly looked drawn and weary. "My father was so obsessed with that name, with controlling every design, every product that bore the Colette label, that it tore my family apart. I left Youngsville more than thirty years ago with the man I loved—a man of whom my parents didn't approve. My father never spoke to me again. No, believe me when I say the name Colette holds no special place in my heart."

"I'm sorry." The words seemed inadequate in the face

of the sad statement. Then another facet of the words caught at him. "If you were disowned, how did you come to be the only remaining family member holding stock? And why didn't your parents keep a simple majority?"

She shrugged. "Before my father died, he sold some stock, assuming that there would be no heir to inherit. But after he passed away, my mother begged me to come back and take over." She snorted. "As if I'd want to." Then she gave him a bittersweet smile. "Still, I couldn't turn her down altogether so I told her I would vote the remaining stock. I still held enough that until you came along and bought more, there was no danger of anyone else making board decisions."

"So you came back here…and that's when you met Sylvie."

Her expression eased into a genuine smile. "Yes. She was special to me from the very beginning. So vibrant, so bright and inquisitive—and doing her best to hide it beneath a bad attitude and tough behavior."

"She's lucky she has you," he said quietly.

"I'm lucky, too," Rose told him and there was a distinctly meaningful tone in her next words. "Sylvie does nothing halfway. Once she lets someone into her heart, they stay there forever. She's made lifelong friends among her co-workers."

He smiled at the older woman, unsure of how he should respond to that. "Sylvie's very special."

He took his leave of her then and returned to Sylvie's bedside. She'd fallen asleep again. He tucked the blankets around her shoulders, seeing the fragile sweep of dark eyelashes on porcelain skin, and a wave of tenderness like nothing he'd ever experienced before swept through him. Abruptly, he could hear Rose's words in his head again: *Once she lets someone into her heart, they stay there forever.* And the panic he'd felt when he'd seen her lying there on the ground shot through him anew. Had Sylvie let him into her heart? He thought that probably she had, and a fierce pleasure at the idea warred with an equally insistent need to flee as far and as fast as he could.

Slowly, he backed out of the room and sank into a chair in her small living room. This wasn't good. She was getting to him in a way no woman ever had. It was an unnerving thought. His life was humming along just fine without the deep emotions that had torn his parents apart. Unwillingly, his father's defeated features swam into his head. After the fiasco with the fake emeralds, the knowledge that her family had been right, that he wasn't good enough for Isadora had been too humiliating and depressing for Frank Grey to get past. Marcus could still hear his mother pleading, begging with her husband not to go, but Frank's self-esteem wouldn't let him stay. He'd died, a broken man in a prison of his own choosing, when Marcus was eighteen and Marcus had seen the small hopeful light that his mother had nursed through the years of her broken marriage fade and die, as well.

No, he thought grimly, he was better off without that kind of emotion in his life. He had no intention of becoming anyone's doormat, or of caring so much for a woman that she would have the power to destroy him if she left. It had taken his mother more than a decade to get herself together again after her marriage disintegrated.

He stood, reaching for his jacket. He didn't *need* Sylvie in his life, he insisted to himself although he'd certainly been enjoying her company. Yes, he was totally hot for her. And he'd feel protective toward any woman who'd been injured. That's all it was. But just so she didn't get the wrong idea, he'd better be careful about how much time he spent with her in the future. It wouldn't be good for her to believe there could be anything lasting between them. They could still have a scorching affair that would get this need he thought he felt for her out of his system, and then he'd get back to normal.

But he carefully avoided his own image in the small hall mirror as he closed her door behind him.

Seven

Three days later, her doorbell rang. He was right on time.

Sylvie tucked her pencil behind her ear and shoved herself away from the paperwork lying all over her small dining table, taking a deep breath to still her jittering nerves. She stopped to check her makeup in the hall mirror—good, still fresh—before taking her sweet time walking to the door and opening it. "Hello, Marcus," she said pleasantly. Ooh, that was good. Not too eager, but not unfriendly.

"Hello, Sylvie."

If only he didn't look so darn good, she thought bitterly. Even though he had a slightly apprehensive air lurking behind his charm, he took her breath away, as he always did when she could feel the intensity of those green eyes focused on her. "Would you like to come in?" She would keep this polite and civil if it killed her.

If this was the way he wanted it, then she would play along. She didn't ever have to see him socially after today. Though the thought brought a sharp lancing pain to pierce her heart, she refused to let it show.

This was the first time he'd come around since he'd brought her home after her accident.

When she'd awakened, he was gone. It had been just as well. Though they each had done their best to remain pleasant and polite, the hours she'd spent with him after her release from the hospital had been stilted and wooden. Unbidden, the words he'd thrown at her in the restaurant echoed in her ears.

All you think about is that precious company...your life would be empty if they fired you tomorrow. He was wrong. If the doors of Colette failed to open one day, or if she lost her job, she'd still have the most precious thing she'd acquired in her years there: her friends. But Marcus couldn't understand that. He didn't understand *her*. He would never fight to the death for a friend, couldn't even imagine why anyone would want to, she supposed.

She'd been stupid, she reminded herself for the millionth time. Stupid to hope that she could ever have a...a permanent relationship with a man as wealthy as Marcus, stupid to think that the two of them could find common ground in their points of view, worse than stupid to have believed, even for a second, that a silly piece of jewelry could have chosen the perfect man for her.

Silently, she stepped back as he entered her apartment. He hadn't called for three days and she'd told herself she was glad he was letting the relationship die. It would be far less awkward than a dissection of the whole miserable mess. She'd get over him.

Okay. That was a lie. But she *would* get over the sick feeling in the pit of her stomach every time she thought about the future without him. She was a self-sufficient, independent person and that had suited her fine. But she'd let her guard down, she'd let him get too close and now she was paying the price. It might take her a long time to stop caring for him, but she would, she promised herself. She *would*.

And she'd been getting a start on it.

Then this afternoon, she'd gotten a phone call from him, asking if she would like to go out to dinner this evening. Though the mere sound of his voice set nerve endings into a wild dance inside her, she forced herself to ignore the longing that urged her to say yes. This man had broken her heart! With a far-too-satisfying insincerity, she'd declined, citing a lot of work she was bringing home. Which wasn't a lie, either. She *did* have a lot of work. But when he'd said he'd like to stop by, she hadn't been able to think of a good reason to refuse without getting into an unpleasant discussion.

His big body brushed by her and she shivered as he moved past, wishing she was anywhere but here. Then he turned and handed her a small bouquet of pink, apricot and yellow roses he'd been carrying. "Here. I thought you might like these."

Yellow roses. For friendship, as everyone knew. Well, that certainly let her know where she stood. Barely glancing at them, she said, "Thank you." She laid the bouquet carelessly on the hall table and smiled at him innocently. "So. What can I do for you?"

He shrugged, smiling, though his eyes were watchful. "I wanted to see you. I've missed you."

She gritted her teeth against the urge to scream *whose fault is that?* Throughout the past several sleepless nights, she'd repeated her mantra over and over again: *It won't work.* A relationship with Marcus was never going to work for her. They were simply too different. He clearly was interested in an easy sexual liaison that didn't demand anything more of him, one that worked according to whatever timetable he happened to be on. One that had nothing to do with the rest of his life, including the way he gobbled up smaller businesses like so much candy. She, on the other hand, wanted more than that. Too much more. Her heart contracted with a vicious squeeze of agony and she had to force herself not to let it show.

"Well," she said brightly, "I've been busy and I'm sure you have been, too."

He nodded. There was a small silence.

She absolutely refused to break it. She was under no obligation to make him feel comfortable. So she just kept her bright smile plastered in place and waited him out.

"How's your head?"

"Fine."

"Good. I was concerned."

So why didn't you call? Her anger rose, steadily feeding her determination to end her association with him.

"I'm sorry you weren't able to have dinner," he said. "Is there another night that would suit?"

She took a deep breath. "No," she said quietly. "There really isn't."

Something heated in the depths of his eyes and a muscle leaped in his jaw. "Why not? I enjoy your company and I thought you enjoyed mine."

"'Company' is the operative word," she informed him, linking her fingers tightly. "Your company is destroying my employer. *That's* why I'm not having dinner with you."

"That's ridiculous," he said sharply.

All right. She'd had it. She could feel the temper rushing to a boil, overruling the cool distance with which she'd resolved to end this. "It's equally ridiculous to categorize the relationship we've been developing as *enjoyable*." Her voice rose and she took a deep breath. "To me, it was a whole lot more than that! You and I...we're looking for different things in life. You're not the kind of man I'm looking for, and I *know* I'm unsuitable for you."

"We aren't unsuitable for each other." His voice was steely and controlled. "In fact, I think we're extremely *well* suited."

"Could have fooled me," she said bitterly. She made a dismissive gesture. "Just take your friendly yellow roses and *go!*"

But he shook his head. "You and I have a powerful connection. You said you wanted to make love with me—"

"Not anymore," she said coldly.

"Oh, really?" His voice was a deep and dangerous growl. Too late, she realized a man like Marcus would take that as a challenge.

"I am done talking to you," she said, pointing to the door with all the authority she could muster. "Goodbye."

"I'm done talking to you, too." He grabbed her extended arm and with one quick tug, dragged her against him.

"Marc—!" But that quickly, his lips were on hers. His arms wrapped around her, trapping her against the hard strength of his body while his mouth moved ravenously, persuasively, aggressively, his tongue plunging deep into her mouth and demanding a response. He was hot, burning her alive with the force of his passion as one hand swept down her body and arched her against him.

She was still squirming and trying to shove him away,

to little effect, when he lifted his head and said, "Be still," in a deep, rough voice.

And she did.

She couldn't have explained it. It wasn't as if she were a pliant, clingy little woman who took orders well. But there was a firm note of command in his tone that stopped her struggles. Frozen, hanging in his arms, she could feel his chest rise and fall in the rapid rhythm of his breathing. His heartbeat thudded through him and into her, and her own body tingled with rising need for him. In a blinding instant of clarity, she knew what she wanted.

She wanted *him.* Why was she fooling herself? She wanted to make love with him at least once before their impossible attraction shattered and broke apart, as she knew it must. She wanted to give him all of her love in the only way he would ever accept it, wanted to taste the heady wine of sensual fulfillment that his kisses promised. She'd never met a man who made her feel the things that Marcus did. And she knew, with a terrible, irrevocable certainty, that she never would again.

His green eyes bored into hers, blazing with sexual promise. He opened his mouth to break the tableau but she forestalled him by simply lifting one hand from his chest and placing her fingers against his lips.

"Shhh." She let her body relax in his arms. At the same time, she slipped her arms up around his broad shoulders, pulling herself closer to him. "Kiss me," she whispered.

To her surprise, he hesitated. She could feel the sexual tension vibrating through him but he didn't move to consolidate his position. "This won't end with kissing," he warned her, his voice still dark-edged. "If it isn't what you want, tell me now."

Warmth blossomed. Even now, at the moment when

he could have simply taken all she offered, he gave her a choice. Acknowledged her need to make that choice, though she had fully acknowledged it herself only moments ago. Tightening her fingers on his shoulders, she lifted her face to his and brushed a small, sweet kiss across his mouth. "It's what I want," she confirmed.

He threaded one hand through her hair and cupped her scalp in his palm, holding her head as he returned the light kiss with a far more potent, powerful one that made her moan and slide her fingers up to caress his nape. Bending, he slipped one arm beneath her knees and lifted her easily into his arms as she clung to him, burying her face in the gilt curls that showed in the vee of his sweater.

He strode down the wide hallway without pausing, and she remembered that he'd been in her bedroom once before—alone. This time, she thought, he wouldn't be alone. And when he was gone, and she was the one who was left alone, she'd have this memory to hold against the loneliness and pain. It wouldn't be enough, but it would have to do.

The thoughts made her respond to him urgently, returning his kisses as he let her slide down to stand beside the bed. He undressed her with sure, competent hands, running his palms over her body possessively before laying her down on the bed and shedding his own clothing. She was relieved when he produced a condom because the thought of birth control hadn't even occurred to her.

He was gentle with her, and she was grateful that he had believed her when she told him she wasn't experienced. He treated her as he might have if she'd truly been a virgin, stroking her, pressing kisses everywhere, his mouth producing streamers of pleasure that soon had her twisting against him, urging him on. And when he lowered himself to her and slowly entered her, there was no pain, only a throbbing pressure that somehow fed the flames of her desire even more.

She clung to him, wrapping her legs around him, clutching him to her with damp, frantic fingers, thrilling to his groans of pleasure as his heavy body surged against her in the final moments of his release. When he rolled to his side and pulled her into the warm cove of his arms a few minutes later, her heart nearly burst with a roiling mixture of love, happiness…and a cutting devastation as she realized how fleeting these moments had been.

It wasn't until the morning that he realized something was wrong.

Sylvie had woken in his arms. He'd carried her into the shower and made love to her again, the water beating down on his back as he pinned her against the wall. He'd spread his palms over her full, pretty breasts, catching her earlobe between his teeth and biting gently as she'd moaned for him. Her face had glowed as she'd lifted it to his. She'd wrapped her legs around him, and he'd had a momentary flashback to the day they'd met, when she'd walked away from him and he'd assessed those legs with automatic male approval. He'd known even then that he wanted her. She'd intrigued him with her sassy manner that covered an enormous soft streak as well as the iron will and drive that got things accomplished. And the more he'd learned, the more interested he'd become.

And now…now here they were. Lovers.

But something wasn't right. He couldn't put his finger on it. There was simply an amorphous cloud hanging over his head, dimming his happiness just the smallest bit. Sylvie was pert and happy, as he'd expected she would be. But once or twice he'd caught her looking at him with an odd expression. She closed her eyes briefly, then stared at him again almost as if she were trying to memorize his features.

He'd called his valet and had him bring over fresh clothing, then started breakfast while Sylvie dressed and dried her hair. She had eggs and bacon, which he figured meant she ate the stuff, so that's what he made.

She came into the kitchen as he slid the eggs onto a plate, and he smiled at her. "Perfect timing."

She slid into her chair, smiling back and her face was so radiant he wondered if he'd been wrong about the hint of reserve he'd sensed. "I've never had a man cook for me before."

"Good," he said with satisfaction as he sat down opposite her. "You'll never forget this, then."

"No." She looked down at her plate, still smiling though he thought her expression dimmed just the smallest bit. "I'll never forget you."

His hand stilled on his fork. That had sounded a bit too definite to him. His comment had been careless, reflexive. Not meant to be important. "Sylvie—"

The doorbell rang.

He swore, with such feeling that her head jerked up and she stared at him, plainly shocked.

"I'll get it," he said. "That will be my valet." He left her sitting there, still staring, as he went downstairs to meet his man at the locked front entrance. When he returned, she was rinsing her plate and stacking things in the dishwasher.

"I'm sorry to rush out on you," she said, "but I have a ton of work waiting for me. Take your time, stay as long as you like. Just lock the doors behind you."

"What kind of work?"

"Uh, planning that new campaign. I'll be working on

it all week.'' She angled her head and eyed him curiously as she went to get her coat and briefcase. ''Why?''

Well, damn it, he didn't really know why. But for some reason, he badly wanted to be able to envision her in her office, to think about her and know what she was working on. ''I'd like to see it,'' he said slowly. As alarm flared in her eyes, he hastily added, ''Not to make changes. I just want to see what you do.''

Her eyes widened a fraction and her smile bloomed. Then, as if someone had whispered something unpleasant in her ear, the expression dimmed to a merely pleasant stretching of the lips. Walking toward him, she stretched up and casually kissed him before heading out the door. ''That would be lovely. Come by anytime.''

He meant to go that very day, but when he arrived at his own office, there was a stack of messages and urgent duties that kept him occupied all of Monday. And he had a business dinner that evening.

Near five o'clock, he called Sylvie. When she answered, he said, ''I have a business dinner tonight that might run late so I won't be able to see you.''

There was no response but he could sense the question in her silence.

''I thought you…should know.''

There was still a hesitation on the line. Then she said, ''Thank you. That was considerate.'' There was a distinct note of surprise in her voice, as if she hadn't expected him to think of her.

It annoyed him, although he'd been the one who'd insisted he wasn't getting involved with her on more than a physical level. *Serves me right,* he thought wryly. Then he spoke again. ''I have to go out of town tomorrow and I'll be back sometime Thursday. Would you like to get together Thursday evening?''

"Um...I guess." She sounded so hesitant he started to sweat.

"You don't sound sure," he said. Every male instinct in his body was screaming at him, telling him to forget his work and go to her *now*. Imprint himself on her so thoroughly that she'd know she belonged to him, make sure she understood just how completely she belonged to him now.

"I'd like that very much." Her voice was warmer now. "Would you like to come over for dinner? I believe it's my turn to cook for you."

"That would be great." And this time he'd bring along a few things so that he wouldn't have to call his damn valet in the morning. He lowered his voice when he spoke again. "Take care of yourself, sweetheart. I'll see you in two days."

"All right." Her voice was quiet.

"Will you miss me?"

He heard her huff out a breath, and he couldn't decide whether it was distress at his leaving or exasperation at him for prolonging the interruption in her day. Then she said, "I'll miss you very much," and the note of longing in her voice made him relax in satisfaction.

"Good," he said. "I'll miss you, too."

He called her at work on Tuesday when he arrived in Toledo and felt better just because he'd heard her voice. On Wednesday, he told himself he wasn't calling her. He hadn't made any rash promises this time that she could misinterpret. But at nine that evening, lying on his hotel bed wishing she were there beside him—no, *beneath him* would be a whole lot better—he gave in to the thoughts of her that constantly circled in his head.

When she said hello, the tension inside him subsided so fast that his limbs felt leaden. "Hi."

"Marcus!" Her voice rose in unmistakable delight. Then she quickly moderated her tone. "Is your business going well?"

"It went fine. I'll be flying home tomorrow and—" he dropped his voice to suit his next words, "I'll be holding you this time tomorrow night."

She made a small, soft sound that made his body stir in response. "Hurry home," she said in a throaty purr.

He laughed, but even he could hear the note of desperation in it. "I wish I was there with you now."

"I wish you were, too."

Then he told her, in dark, sensual detail exactly what he'd like to be doing, until his own body was throbbing and he could hear her quickened breathing even through the phone connection. "…And when we recover, we'll start all over again," he finally concluded.

"You," she accused in a breathless tone, "are a very, very bad man. Now how am I supposed to sleep after that?"

"As badly as I've slept without you in my arms." The silence was immediate and he wasn't sure who was more shocked, her or himself.

Then her voice came to him one more time. "I'll see you tomorrow evening."

His flight got in around three-thirty the next afternoon. Marcus had intended to go by his own office, but as he got into the waiting car, he directed his driver to the Colette building. He couldn't wait until this evening to see her.

Once at the jewelry company, he strode through the outer offices, leaving startled receptionists in his wake.

He didn't give them his destination; he wanted to surprise Sylvie. He knew approximately where her office was because he'd looked it up right after they'd first met.

Her door was standing open as he approached. He stepped into the room, looking around for her.

"Marcus!" She was seated at her desk and as their eyes met and held, she launched herself out of her chair, and into his embrace, throwing her arms around his neck and hugging tightly. Then, as she realized where she was, she started to draw back.

But he was in no mood to let her go. "Kiss me," he said, hauling her up against him with one hand and threading the other through her hair, cradling her scalp as he pulled her head back and set his lips on hers. She made a muffled sound but she met him joyously, opening her mouth to his searching tongue, letting him take her as deep and as thoroughly as he dared in a public building. Her hands caressed his shoulders and back, and her slim, rounded figure felt so good against him he wished he could snap his fingers and transport them instantly to a private place.

When he finally lifted his mouth from hers, she said, "I'm so glad you're home!" and for the first time since he'd met her, since he'd known he wanted her, for the first time in his entire life, the world felt perfect to him.

"I'm glad I'm home, too." He barely recognized his own voice. He cleared his throat and let her slide down to the floor again, grimacing as he fought the arousal that the feel of her moving over him produced. "Can you leave now?"

An expression of dismay crossed her mobile features and her soft brown eyes were distressed. "I can't," she said regretfully, tugging down her silky sweater and tossing her hair out of the way.

"Sure? Your work can wait until tomorrow, can't it?" He caught her hand.

"It's not work." Her gaze traveled over his face as if she wanted to assure herself he was really there, and when he reached for her other hand, she let him take it. "My friend Maeve is here."

"And?" He didn't get it.

Her face lit up again. "Oh, I forgot, you haven't met Maeve." She started across the room, tugging him along in her wake. "I promised I'd help Maeve in the ladies' room before she and Wil leave today."

He still didn't understand. Wil, he knew, was her boss, Wil Hughes. But as she opened a side door and took him into the adjoining office to introduce him to Wil's wife, he realized what she meant.

Maeve Hughes was in a wheelchair. She was an attractive, fiftyish woman and she was warm and enthusiastic when Sylvie introduced them. Her husband looked vaguely familiar and he assumed that the man had been at or near one of the management meetings he'd held.

"Sylvie tells me you've been out of town," Maeve said.

"Yes, and I'm happy to be back." He'd released Sylvie's hand earlier but he sent her a private smile.

When he looked back at Maeve, her eyebrows were raised and she was exchanging a significant glance with her husband. Well, he didn't care who knew about Sylvie and him. In fact, he wanted people to know she was involved with him now. She was his. The thought flooded him with a primitive satisfaction. He didn't fully understand it, but he didn't care. He was here, with Sylvie, and soon they would be at her apartment, in her big iron bed, making love like he'd dreamed of doing for three days straight.

After a few moments of small talk, Sylvie and Maeve excused themselves and left the room. There was a tentative silence in their wake.

"I understand Sylvie's developed a new ad campaign," Marcus said. Hughes seemed so awkward and uncomfortable that Marcus thought he ought to throw the man a line.

"Yes." Wil brightened. "She's done a marvelous job. Would you like to see it?"

Marcus followed Sylvie's boss back into her office and over to an easel standing in the corner.

"This is the presentation she made to the whole department today," Wil told him. "It's for the Everlasting collection, our newly designed line of engagement and wedding rings. When I asked who wanted this project, Sylvie fought for it. One of her closest friends, Meredith Blair, designed it. Sylvie thinks the rings are gorgeous and her admiration surely comes through in this ad plan."

"I didn't realize she was so intimately involved in the creation of the campaigns," Marcus said. "I assumed that as your assistant, she would be overseeing other staff most of the time." The ads she'd planned were striking, using pale pink roses, a woman in a flowing, gauzy wedding dress and a model-handsome man as the motif carried through each frame.

"She isn't always in on the design process," Wil said. He gave Marcus a droll look. "But if you know Sylvie at all, you know she's not one to stand on the sidelines. I have to let her in on the action once or twice a year or she'll make my life miserable."

Marcus grinned. "I understand perfectly."

A phone rang in Wil's office as they were chuckling. "Excuse me, please," he said as he disappeared through the adjoining door.

Marcus stayed at the easel, flipping through Sylvie's work. She was amazingly talented. Wil might laugh about keeping her happy, but it was obvious she had a true genius for her work.

Just then, a young redheaded woman came barreling into the office. "Hey, Sylvie, guess what I—" She stopped short, mouth open as she stared at Marcus. After what seemed like a long time but really was just a moment, the woman recovered. Stepping forward, she held out a tentative hand. "Hello, Mr. Grey. I'm sorry if I've disturbed you. I was just looking for Sylvie."

How the devil did all these people recognize him on sight? Then he sighed. He supposed if someone was trying to acquire the company for whom he'd worked and if it were rumored that his job hung in the balance, he'd know everything there was to know about that someone. "Hello."

"Do you, uh, know where Sylvie went?" The redhead's nervousness was palpable.

"She's with Wil's wife at the moment. I'm sure she'll soon be back, if you'd like to wait."

"That's okay. I'll catch her tomorrow." She started to back out of the room.

"Could I give her a message?" Marcus asked politely. What he really wanted to do was bellow, "I'm not the enemy!"

"No, no, it wasn't important." The young woman held up a piece of paper she'd been holding and Marcus realized it was a photo. "I just wanted to give her the Christmas photo we had taken of our girls. They're six and four. Sylvie sometimes baby-sits them and the kids think she's fantastic."

"Most people do," Marcus said dryly.

The woman's face softened and she smiled. "Yeah,

that's true." Then Sylvie's co-worker turned and made a beeline for the door. "Nice, uh, meeting you, sir. Like I said, I'll see her tomorrow." And she vanished.

"I'm not your enemy," Marcus muttered aloud.

Then he stopped, his hand frozen on the easel page he was about to turn. No, he might not be their enemy, but they thought he was. He'd even thought it himself a few minutes ago. *His* job wasn't on the line if this company changed hands.

Slowly, he let his arm drop to his side. Sylvie had made her point, he thought, but he couldn't be annoyed, because she didn't even know she'd done it. She'd introduced him to people from her world—and her world was Colette. Her friends *were* Colette.

Wil, with his wife in a wheelchair. Marcus knew Maeve would have trouble getting health insurance anywhere else if Wil lost his job. Jim and the nameless young woman who'd just rushed out, working to support families, were also Sylvie's friends.

Colette wasn't *his* enemy, either, he realized, feeling the lifting of an invisible weight from his heart. His mother had told him the truth about the emerald swindle that had ruined his father. It hadn't been Carl Colette's fault. Those workers who had left Van Arl and gone to work for Colette had been trying to support families, care for loved ones, make a living. It had been unfortunate. No more, no less.

His father had been his own worst enemy, Marcus thought with another flash of insight. Why had he allowed pride to tear his family apart? His wife would have loved him no matter what. *Had* loved him, he thought, remembering all the years his mother had clung to the hope that his father would come to his senses some day.

He thought of how far he'd come since the day of the

board meeting at which he'd met Sylvie. When he'd walked into that room that morning, he'd been on the verge of shutting the doors of Colette. True, he would have offered the employees chances to work for Grey Enterprises, but many of those jobs would have involved cross-country moves. He'd have uprooted dozens of families for no better reason than a thirst for revenge.

Now...now he had a much better idea. He wouldn't close Colette. There was no reason to. The company's stock had been a little soft even before he'd become involved with it—the board hadn't been the wisest group of managers. But with him at the helm, Colette could maintain the fine name it had always had.

He'd take a few days to consider all the legal ramifications before he said anything to Sylvie. He knew her well—she'd have a million questions, and he'd better make sure he had answers. But he couldn't imagine that a merger in which Colette would become a division of Grey Enterprises while still retaining a certain amount of autonomy would be anathema to her.

His mind was spinning with new ideas and when Sylvie came back into the office a few minutes later, he greeted her so exuberantly that she said, "Why are you so happy?"

Laughing, he hugged her around the shoulders. "I'm with you," he said. "Why wouldn't I be happy?"

He drove her home, holding her hand the whole way, reluctant to let go of her even for that short a distance. His body felt jittery with anticipation, and the moment her door closed behind them, he hauled her up against him.

"Kiss me," he growled. "I haven't been able to think of anything but you all week."

Her eyes widened and her pretty smile bloomed. Sliding her hands around his waist inside his opened coat, she lifted her mouth to his, pressing herself against him as she let him take her deep into the passion he'd been waiting for.

Waiting for too long, he realized, as the blood roared in his head and his hips surged heavily against hers. He pushed her coat off her shoulders and shrugged out of his, still kissing her. Then he wrapped his arms around her, palming her curving bottom and pulling her fully up against him. She gasped, and the small sound inflamed his senses even more, drowning all awareness of the world around them. His world, at this moment, was Sylvie, and the sweet fulfillment her soft body promised.

He tore her blouse open in one swift motion, ignoring her shocked cry and the buttons that flew everywhere, lifting one perfect ivory breast from its silk-and-lace confinement and tugging at the nipple for a moment before placing his mouth on the taut rosy peak and suckling strongly. Her hands came up into his hair, holding him against her as her fingers flexed on his scalp. Then they slid down, loosening his tie and unbuttoning his shirt until she could slide her hands beneath and run them over the hard planes of his shoulders and chest.

He groaned at the erotic sensation of her small hands rushing over him. He was so aroused his pants were a painful constriction and he circled her wrist with one big hand, drawing hers down to the fastening of his pants. She froze for a moment, and he remembered how new all this was to her. But then her fingers began to fumble with his belt buckle, work at the clasp of his trousers, tug at the zipper. Now it was his turn to groan as she brushed over the rigid flesh he couldn't hide. He felt her tugging at his clothes and in one sudden, bold move, she freed him, her small fingers pushing away the fabric before lightly exploring.

He groaned again, thrusting himself into her palm. But after only a moment of the wonderful, too-arousing sensation, he pulled her hand away. Dragging handfuls of her skirt out of the way, he tugged her to the floor, hooking his hand in her panty hose and panties and ruthlessly yanking her free of them. He knelt between her white thighs, looking down at the succulent feast he'd exposed, and when his gaze traveled to her face, he saw she was blushing. As their eyes met, she held out her arms.

Wordlessly, he came into her embrace, sliding into her slick, warm body easily, knowing even as he began a sweet, solid rhythm, driving himself home, that it wasn't going to last nearly long enough to satisfy him.

Eight

Marcus had asked her to meet him for lunch on Wednesday of the following week. So at twenty minutes before twelve, Sylvie walked down the long hallway toward Marcus's office, humming beneath her breath. The building was festive, ready for the holidays with muted carols playing over the sound system and holiday decorations draping every office doorway. She walked slowly, admiring the display. She was early, but that was okay. He'd seen her workplace; she was curious about his as well.

Her body still felt tender and tingly from the long hours of lovemaking that had recurred throughout the night before. She'd never dreamed she could feel the things Marcus made her feel, and she felt her cheeks grow hot at the mere memory of some of those astounding pleasures he had shown her in recent days. Her feet slowed as she neared the door to which she'd been directed, a ridiculous shyness seizing her.

He hadn't let her sleep alone a single night since their first cataclysmic lovemaking...

"—want to initiate the Colette paperwork as soon as possible."

She paused as she recognized Marcus's voice. *What Colette paperwork?* Her pace slowed to a complete halt. A slight chill rippled over her as the words began to make sense, and she shivered involuntarily.

"All right. Shall I call a board meeting?" The voice was feminine, presumably an office assistant.

"No. There's only one other stockholder in the company now. I'll discuss it with her before we present it to the board. That way, we'll have all our ducks in a row and no one will be able to raise any objections."

Sylvie pressed a hand against her mouth, stifling the cry of anguish that threatened to escape. *Marcus was going ahead with his plans to liquidate Colette.* Her heart, so light a moment earlier, became a leaden weight in her breast. Though they carefully hadn't discussed it since her accident on the ice, she had been sure that Marcus had changed his mind. His own mother had explained to him that he was wrong to blame Colette for his father's undoing. Hadn't he heard anything she'd said?

Apparently not, she thought dully. Inside the man she loved was a little boy who'd been hurt beyond belief when his family—his world—fell apart. And no amount of explanation could erase his thirst for revenge, no matter how misguided it might be.

He didn't love her. The thought cut like a newly sharpened blade.

Though she'd reminded herself of that in the days since they'd first made love, her heart hadn't believed it.

He had been so tender with her, had seemed to need to be in frequent contact, had wanted to spend every night together. He hadn't told her he loved her, but she'd been able to tell.

Or so she'd thought.

Quickly, she spun and began to retreat down the hallway. There was a women's room near the elevator and she ducked into it, relieved to find it deserted. Turning the lock, she sank into the lounging sofa along one wall and dropped her head into her hands. *What was she going to do?* She couldn't stay with him, pretend nothing was wrong, when her heart was breaking.

This is your own fault, she told herself fiercely. He'd never said he was going to abandon his plans for Colette. He'd never said he understood her devotion, or that he'd stop organizing a takeover. In fact, he'd never talked to her at all about it, never shared his feelings on the subject except under extreme duress. Tears stung her eyes and she pressed her palms hard against them, refusing to give in to the tears that threatened.

When the cell phone in her purse rang, she leaped a foot in the air. With trembling fingers, she pulled it out and flipped it open. "Hello?"

"Hello, sweetheart. Are you on your way?"

She froze. *Marcus.* Without thinking, she punched the button and cut him off, then leaped to her feet and bolted for the elevator. She had just walked out the front door of Grey Enterprises when her phone rang again. She ignored it. Hailing a taxi, she climbed in and gave the driver her home address, then opened her phone again and called Wil.

When she explained that she needed the rest of the day off, he agreed easily. Then he said, "Ah, Sylvie, are you all right?"

"Of course." She worked hard to keep her voice even. "I just have a million things to get done before the holidays and I realized I'm running out of time."

"What shall I tell Marcus when he calls?"

The question caught her off guard. "I, ah—"

"Because he's already called once," Wil added. "I told him I thought you had gone to lunch."

She closed her eyes. Rats. Focusing again, she said lightly, "I'll call him now so he stops trying to track me down. He shouldn't need to call you again."

She ended the conversation, aware that her hands were shaking. With reluctant fingers, she punched in the Grey Enterprises number, then dialed Marcus's extension when the automated voice system came on.

"Marcus Grey." His voice was deep and preoccupied.

"Marcus—"

"Sylvie!" His tone sharpened. "Where are you? I tried to call you a few minutes ago but I got cut off and then I couldn't get through. Are you on your way over?"

"No." She cleared her throat. "I'm not going to be able to make it."

"But I just talked to Wil and he said you were going to lunch. Is everything all right?"

"Everything's fine. I've just—something's come up and I'm going to have to go out of town for a few days. I'll call you when I get back."

"Out of town?" He sounded distinctly skeptical. "Work related?"

"No," she managed, hating the lie but knowing she wasn't strong enough for the scene he would create when she told him the truth. "An old friend needs me."

There was a short silence. "I see." Then his tone softened. "Sylvie to the rescue again, hmm? All right, sweetheart, but call me as soon as you can."

"All right. Sorry, I'm losing your signal. Goodbye." She shut off the phone again as the cab pulled up in front of Amber Court.

After paying the cabby, she rushed upstairs. The old mansion was silent in the middle of the day. Most of the people who lived there had day jobs. And Rose probably was off doing volunteer work somewhere. *Or working for the caterer.* Sylvie winced as she realized how completely she'd dropped the ball on that one. She'd meant to get some of the other tenants together and tell them what she'd discovered. But in the tumultuous few weeks since Marcus had come into her life, she'd simply forgotten.

She let herself into her apartment, dropping her bag and her coat uncharacteristically on the floor as she wandered through her home. *What was she going to do?* She couldn't imagine staying in Youngsville now, couldn't imagine where her relationship with Marcus was headed. She'd known from the very beginning that they weren't right for each other, but she'd allowed her heart to argue her out of her common sense. And though she'd made love to him the first time knowing that it couldn't last, the past week had lulled her into believing that anything was possible.

But it wasn't. The tears she'd suppressed earlier began to fall, faster and faster, as she realized the only way to survive this now was for her to leave. But…where could she go? She'd never lived anywhere but Youngsville, except for the two years when she'd transferred from Youngsville Community College to Indiana State. And the day she'd graduated, she'd come home again because she'd already gotten the offer from Colette. Offer…

A recent memory popped into her head, as if it had been waiting behind a closed door that had just been

opened. San Diego! Four months ago, before she'd ever
met Marcus, she'd attended a jewelry exhibition in that
city, at which Colette had featured some of their new
designs. A man had come by the Colette booth and she'd
struck up a conversation. It wasn't until he'd given her
his business card that she'd realized that he was one of
the top jewelry designers in the country. And here she'd
been lecturing him about aggressive marketing strategies.
She could have sunk through the floor. But the man,
Charles Martin, apparently had been impressed. He'd
come by the booth again the following day as they were
striking the display and made her a job offer. A very
generous one.

A job offer! She'd been astounded. And flattered,
though she'd explained that she was very happy with
Colette. But Mr. Martin had patted her hand when she'd
gently refused and told her to call him if she ever
changed her mind.

Before she could list all the reasons why a hasty move
would be crazy, she reached for her business card file
and the telephone. Ten minutes later, she had an interview scheduled for Friday and was making airline reservations. She'd leave town on a late flight today and
spend a couple of days in San Diego. Her heart might be
broken, she told herself stoutly as she dialed her boss's
extension to arrange for the time off, but she refused to
allow herself to crawl into bed and pull the covers over
her head.

Which was what she longed to do. After she'd hung
up with Wil, and as she pulled her suitcase from the back
of her closet and began throwing things into it in a very
un-Sylvie-like fashion, the tears came again. And this
time, she threw herself on the bed and let herself grieve
for the death of all her dreams.

* * *

"Where in the hell have you been?"

Marcus stood in Sylvie's doorway on Sunday afternoon, as angry as he could remember being in…well, *ever*. He had filled her answering machine with messages to call him, as well as her cell phone, which she'd apparently left behind when she went to California.

"San Diego. How did you know I was home?" In contrast to his rage, she was subdued and strangely flat. Not her normal bouncy self at all. And she was avoiding his eyes.

"I've been calling Rose every hour or so." He speared her with another angry gaze. "Care to share with me the reason you haven't bothered calling in four days?"

She shrugged. "I'm sorry. I was very busy and I guess I just forgot."

"Uh-huh." He hadn't fallen off the turnip truck yesterday. Striding forward, he backed her into the kitchen, trapping her against the counter as he leaned forward, deliberately menacing. "Tell me another one. Two people who share the kind of circuit-frying sex we do don't simply *forget*."

"All *right*." She frowned and ducked under his arm. "Stop shouting at me," she said with the first hint of the old Sylvie he'd seen. She took a deep breath and sighed, and the mournful note in the sound sent a shiver of apprehension through him. "You might as well sit down. I have something to tell you."

He hesitated, unnerved more than he liked by the tone of her voice. "What?"

"Sit down," she repeated. She walked past him into the living room and perched on the edge of a chair.

Slowly, he followed. He'd rather have sat on the sofa with an arm around her, but she was prickly and defiant.

He supposed he shouldn't have shouted at her. After all, hadn't he done the exact same thing once, not call her? His heart sank as he remembered his defensive reasoning. But that was weeks ago, when he'd still been trying to pretend that he didn't have anything more than a casual, fun-filled dalliance in mind. Sylvie didn't have that excuse. Did she?

Sylvie took another deep breath, distracting him. "Talk," he ordered.

She closed her eyes and laced her fingers together, then opened them and he saw grim resolve in her normally sparkling brown eyes. "I'm resigning, effective the end of the year," she said in a rush. "I've taken a job with Martin Gems in San Diego."

He couldn't have heard her right. He let the words sink in but they still sounded the same. "No," he said.

She nodded. "Yes. I'm sorry to have to tell you so abruptly."

He sprang to his feet as helpless fury filled him. "*Why,* damn it? I thought we—you—" He stopped, not sure how to articulate his turbulent thoughts.

She nodded again, but this time it was accompanied by a melancholy smile. "Yes, I know what you thought. You thought I was so enthralled with you that I'd be available whenever, wherever, as long as you wanted me." Although her tone was resigned rather than accusatory, the words stung and he shifted uncomfortably.

"Sylvie—" He fumbled for words. "I thought our...attraction was a mutual thing. What can I say to change your mind? I don't want you to go to San Diego."

"Why?"

The single soft question stopped him cold. "What do you mean, why?" he asked warily.

"Why don't you want me to go?" she repeated patiently. There was an oddly cautious expression on her face, and something that looked like hope flickered to life in her eyes.

He hesitated. And in that long moment of indecision, the small ray of light in her eyes dimmed as clouds of sadness gathered. "I want you to stay," he said haltingly. "I just do. And I know you want to stay with me. We have a good thing," he said, not caring that there was a pleading note in his voice now. "You're making this more complex than it has to be, Sylvie."

She ignored him, rising and walking to the door. "There isn't any point in talking it to death," she said quietly. "My resignation will be on Wil's desk tomorrow."

"There's no need for this." He followed, trying to catch her hand but she put both hands behind her back. "Sylvie, *please* stay."

But she shook her head. "I can't."

Desperate now, he caught her in his arms and bent his head to hers, but she turned her face aside and wouldn't kiss him, wouldn't embrace him. Her body was as rigid as a board in his arms. When she pushed away, he let her go.

"All my life," she said in a barely audible tone. "It's taken me my entire life to realize that I deserve someone to share my life, someone to love and grow old with. I'm not settling for less. Which apparently is all you can offer." Her eyes met his. "I love you, Marcus. I've loved you almost since we met, but I won't beg for your feelings in return. You've walled yourself away behind solid defenses because you're determined never to get hurt again, or to let anyone hurt you like your father hurt your mother. But Marcus, hurting is a part of life experience, a part of loving. You're missing out on so much joy, hiding behind your walls.''

"Sylvie. Sweetheart—''

"No,'' she said with a hint of her normal asperity. "I've let you hurt me, mostly through my own stupidity. I wanted you to be someone you aren't. Someone without human frailties like resentment, someone nobler. So I haven't been fair to you, either. But—'' and she clenched her fists, "I won't let you ruin my life. I *will* get over you,'' she said fiercely.

"But…you just said you loved me—'' Even to his own ears, he sounded pathetic.

"I also just said I'll get over you.'' Her tone was as cold and final as he'd ever heard it, her face stonier than he'd have believed it could be. "Go!''

Stunned by her words, he could only stare as she yanked open the door and gestured for him to leave. His feet moved of their own accord because his brain was whirling, trying to assimilate everything she'd said.

And before he could come up with any meaningful words, he realized her door had closed and he was standing in the hallway, listening to the sound of sobbing from inside her apartment. Numbly, he stood there for a long moment. His instincts told him to break down the door and sweep her into his arms. But for the first time in his life, the predatory instinct that made him such a good businessman was wrong. He knew Sylvie. She had an iron will that more than matched his. A cold chill enveloped his heart. She'd meant what she said, and she wasn't going to let him change her mind.

Slowly, he made his way down the stairs. Rose was standing in the hallway, watering a large potted palm that stood beside the banister. She turned when she saw him coming, silently watching him until he reached her.

"She loves me," he said hoarsely, "but she's leaving. Moving to San Diego."

"Why?" asked Rose.

He stared at her, his brain churning. "I don't know! If she loves me, why would she want to leave me?" He looked at Rose, his eyes burning with an unusual pressure.

Rose looked at him without speaking. She cocked her head slightly and her eyebrows lifted.

Then it hit him, and he sucked in a harsh breath as he stared at Sylvie's friend. "She thinks I don't love her."

Rose folded her arms. "Do you?"

He took a deep breath. He felt like he was about to leap from a plane with no parachute. But wasn't that what Sylvie had just done? It was, he realized, and he'd let her plummet straight to earth without a parachute. "Yes," he said slowly. "I do." His voice grew stronger. "I love her."

Rose smiled and turned back to her watering. "Give her time to get the hurt out of her system and then tell her so."

He turned to bound back up the stairs, then paused, every muscle quivering with frustration. Everything in him urged him to charge back up there and pound on her door until she listened to him. But...Rose had known Sylvie for a long time. "How much time?"

The older woman shrugged. "A day or two, maybe? If you give her too much time to think, you may never get past her defenses."

Give her time to think...that was it! He was almost afraid to let himself hope that the idea he was hatching might work. But as he stood there, his heart aching and his world collapsing as he realized what he'd lost, what he might never be able to regain, he knew he had no choice but to try.

Because if he didn't try, he didn't stand a chance of getting Sylvie back in his arms again.

Slowly, thoughtfully, he said, "Rose? I have a proposal to put to you."

He called Wil Hughes at home that night and told him everything. As Rose had predicted, it wasn't as difficult—or as humiliating—as he'd imagined. Wil only chuckled when Marcus confessed the way he'd hurt Sylvie.

"Someday I'll tell you all the stupid things I did when I was trying to convince Maeve to marry me," the older man said. "Trust me, you're not the first man to have no clue about what a woman is thinking."

When Marcus asked for Wil's help, the older man agreed to his plan without hesitation. "She'll never know that we've spoken," Wil assured him.

As soon as he completed the call, Marcus sank back in his chair and allowed himself the faintest moment of hope. He had set the wheels in motion for what he hoped would be the most momentous meeting of Colette's employees in the history of the company. And if everything went as planned, Sylvie would forgive him.

The first thing she did when she got back into the office on Monday morning was to type and print out her letter of resignation and place it on Wil's desk. Then she set about tackling the mountain of work that had piled up since her precipitous departure the previous Wednesday.

As she'd anticipated, Wil came in moments later, hung up his coat and called a welcome back into her office.

Then he headed down the hall in search of coffee. It wasn't until he returned, revived, that he actually looked at his desk. And a moment later, he was in her office.

"What is this?" He waved her letter in the air hard enough to tear the paper.

Sylvie hesitated. She'd known it was going to be hard. But she hadn't known how hard. Swallowing against the lump that rose in her throat, she said, "I've been offered a job in San Diego. I'm resigning."

"San Diego!" Wil's face registered surprise. "Sylvie, you never mentioned a word about this. Why? Aren't you happy here?"

"Of course I am." She couldn't stop the tears that started but she refused to blink and aid them on their way down her cheeks. "But it's a good offer. One I really can't afford to pass up."

"It's because of the takeover, isn't it?" Wil asked. "Surely you aren't afraid your job will be axed. I can't imagine Marcus firing you."

The tears slid down her cheeks faster. "This has nothing to do with the takeover." She couldn't, in good conscience, tell Wil it had nothing to do with Marcus. "It's—just something I have to do, Wil."

Her boss stared at her accusingly. "Maeve is going to be beside herself when I tell her you're moving to California." His eyes narrowed. "Well, I'm not telling her. You'll have to do your dirty work yourself."

"All right," she whispered. "I'll call her later this afternoon."

"This is awfully sudden," Wil said, glaring at her. "How can you make a snap decision like that?" He shook a finger at her. "I refuse to accept this letter."

That shook her. "But you have to!"

"I do not." He slapped the offending paper down on the corner of her desk.

Abruptly, her tact—and her temper—flew out the window. "Yes," she said angrily, "you do. Because I'm not quitting at the end of the year. I quit *today!*" Standing so quickly her chair flew backward and banged against the credenza behind her desk, she snatched her purse out of the bottom drawer, retrieved her coat and sailed out the door.

She hadn't even gotten to the elevator when she began to calm down enough for the shame to start creeping in. Why had she treated poor Wil like that? It wasn't *him* she was mad at. Mad wasn't even the right word. She was *hurt.* It wasn't Wil who had broken her heart and it wasn't fair of her to treat him badly. Still…a clean break now would be easier. She left the building and began walking briskly toward Amber Court, vowing to call Wil tonight and apologize—but not to take back her decision to resign immediately. She needed to get away quickly.

Leaving was going to be tough enough. Rose and her three closest friends, Meredith, Jayne and Lila, were going to be terribly upset. Hanging around for weeks while they all tried to change her mind would be unbearable.

Yes, she needed a quick, clean break with her old life. Because she knew Marcus. He hated losing, whether it was a business deal or anything else. That was the real reason he'd reacted so strongly to her announcement, she was sure.

She never should have tried to talk to him about leaving. If she'd been thinking, she'd have handled it differently. Marcus was a man used to making decisions, used to being the one in charge. She could picture the brilliant, intense focus in his face when he was making a new deal.

He *hated* losing. And that's how he would perceive

her resignation. He wouldn't want to be the one to whom everyone pointed behind his back and about whom they giggled, the man who'd been dumped by a Colette office employee. She should have waited, should have kept her secret to herself until she could make a single announcement right before she left.

Then the only thing that would have broken would have been her heart.

Nine

She was making a list of the things she'd have to do to get her apartment ready for the next tenant when the phone rang the next morning. Although she was tempted to ignore it, Sylvie forced herself to get to her feet and reach for the handset. She'd spent a sleepless night alternating between black despair and floods of tears. Her throat was raw and her eyes were swollen; she was in no mood to talk to anyone, particularly since she assumed most of her callers would be friends trying to talk her out of leaving Colette and Youngsville.

"Hi, Sylvie." It was Wil.

"Wil. What's up?" She'd called him the night before and apologized. She'd also told Maeve about her new job. What could he want now?

"I just got word that Marcus has called a general meeting of all Colette employees for four o'clock on Monday afternoon."

Sylvie was silent.

"Syl?"

"Why are you telling me this, Wil?" she asked quietly. "I'm no longer a Colette employee."

"Technically, you are," Wil said. "I'm treating your absence as paid leave until your sick and vacation accumulation runs out. By the way, do you realize how much leave you've got coming? Don't you ever take vacations?"

"Rarely." She took a breath. "Wil, I appreciate the gesture, but—"

"Colette needs you," Wil said, and she was surprised by the forceful note in his normally soft tone. "You've been the leader of these people for several months now. You've organized things and kept morale up. How will it look if you aren't there?"

"I can't imagine I'll be missed," she said.

"Don't underestimate yourself." He wasn't giving up. "At least think about it. You're the perfect person to lead a protest right now—since you're leaving and you've already submitted your resignation, they can't fire you. You owe this to your friends at Colette."

She recognized manipulation when she heard it. But still…he did have a valid point. She couldn't just walk away from her responsibilities to all her friends at the company. That was the only reason she would agree to attend. So what if Marcus would be there? It wasn't as if she *needed* to see him one last time. She silently strangled the part of her that quickened at the thought of seeing Marcus. He was in the past now.

She sighed. "All right. I'll be there."

But as she returned to her packing, the phone rang again. This time it was Rose. "Does Monday evening

suit you for dinner? It works for Jayne, Meredith and
Lila.''

"Don't you work at the soup kitchen on Mondays?''
She couldn't think of much she'd rather do less than face
her inquisitive friends.

"Not this week," Rose said cheerily.

"Ah, sure. I guess Monday evening will be fine." She
was dreading telling Rose and everyone else about leaving Indiana. Her friends undoubtedly would hear it
through the office grapevine before she could tell them.
Although it would be an ordeal, their monthly group meal
would be a good time to tell Rose and to explain to them
all; then she'd only have to say it once.

Sunday dragged. She went to church and continued the
tedious, painful task of packing. By the time Monday
afternoon arrived, she was desperate to get her last Colette meeting over with. Part of her was jittery with
nerves at the thought of seeing Marcus again. The other
part of her, the cowardly part, dreaded it. He was the
kind of man who met life head-on. And she seriously
doubted that he'd finished trying to change her mind. He
might have been temporarily stunned into silence when
she'd bluntly booted him out of her apartment on Friday
night, but he'd certainly rebounded by now.

On the other hand, he hadn't called. Hadn't come by.
Maybe he'd accepted her decision. Maybe he was even
relieved by it.

She dressed with care for her farewell meeting in a
simply cut navy suit with white piping that looked
vaguely nautical and did wonderful things for her figure.
If she was going to do this, she was going to do it right,
she thought, looking at her reflection in the long mirror
on the back of her bedroom door.

Rose's brooch lay on her dresser. She hesitated, tracing

a gentle finger over its vaguely heart-shaped surface.
Rose had only been partially correct about its magic. Yes,
she *had* met the only man she could love while wearing
it. But unlike her three friends, she had no happy ending
in sight.

Then she bit down fiercely on her lower lip to keep it
from quivering. *That* wasn't part of the image she wanted
to project. Snatching her hand away from the brooch, she
turned toward the door.

She walked the ten blocks to the Colette building in a
bracing winter wind, then repaired her hair and makeup
in the washroom before taking a deep breath and entering
the conference room behind a couple of stragglers. She
was almost late, just the way she'd planned it. This way,
she hadn't had time to chat with anyone.

Heads turned and smiles lit the faces of her friends and
co-workers as people caught sight of her, and there were
a few low murmurs. By now, she was sure news of her
departure had spread throughout every department. She
hoped no one thought her presence meant she had
changed her mind.

She deliberately didn't look toward the front of the
room as she took a chair in the back beside Meredith,
who'd been wildly waving and signaling that she'd saved
a seat. But as she slid into the row, she heard Marcus's
deep voice as he welcomed everyone and began to speak,
and she forced herself to look up and pretend interest.
He was staring straight at her; for a single moment, she
felt the world spin out of control as his green eyes met
hers and her breathing quickened. *How could she leave
him?* Quickly, she laced her fingers together and dug her
nails into the knuckles of each hand until the pain was
strong enough to grab her attention. She looked away

then, staring fixedly down at her navy leather pumps while he spoke.

"...know that you have heard many rumors about what was going to happen to your company under my management. Today, I intend to share that with you. But first, I'd like to introduce you to the other person who still holds stock in this company, the only surviving member of the Colette family." He walked to a door at the side of the room and opened it, drawing someone into the meeting. "Rose Colette Carson."

Rose Colette Carson. Beside her, Meredith made a sound of shocked surprise and her hand shot out to clutch Sylvie's sleeve. The words took a moment to make sense in her head as she watched her dear friend and landlady walk to the front of the room on Marcus's arm. He led Rose straight to the speaker's podium, where she reached out and adjusted the microphone as if she'd been doing it for years. Rose? Rose *Colette?* Sylvie shook her head slightly.

"Good afternoon, friends," Rose began. "I'm sure this is quite a surprise to all of you."

"Understatement of the millennium," Meredith muttered, releasing her death grip on Sylvie's arm.

"It's a surprise to me, too." Rose's eyes twinkled with that special, knowing look Sylvie knew so well. Then her face sobered. "I left Youngsville—and Colette—many years ago. After my father passed away, I couldn't refuse my mother's pleas to return, although I had no interest in becoming actively involved with the running of the company again. Like you, I was concerned when I learned Grey Enterprises had acquired enough stock to control the company and, like you, I have been apprehensive about the future. But I'm here today to share some very good news." She sent Marcus a beaming smile. "Mr. Grey and I intend to keep Colette in its current condition as a designer of fine jewelry—"

The room erupted in wild cheers.

Rose stopped, smiling, until the noise died down. "However, we also plan to add an additional branch which will offer beautiful, yet more affordable pieces for the general public." Her smile faded. "My philosophy is different from my father's. I believe that everyone should be able to enjoy pleasing jewelry and our new line will promote that." Her voice grew stronger as she spoke, and by the time she was finished, the employees were on their feet again, cheering and whistling as Rose beamed and Marcus came over to give her a warm handshake.

When everyone resumed their seats, Marcus took over the meeting, explaining in more detail the concept they had created and answering questions about the proposed plan. Sylvie carefully didn't look at him again. There was a woman with big Texas hair seated directly in front of her and she slouched a bit so that her view of Marcus was obstructed by that blond mane. Deliberately, she tuned out the sound of those dear, familiar tones and concentrated all her energies on thinking of other things: about what her new job would be like. About Rose and the secret she'd kept for so many years.

It was hard to believe that Rose was part owner of Colette. That Rose *was* a Colette. Sylvie was reluctantly amused when she remembered what she'd been thinking about Rose's dire financial straits. Rose probably could buy and sell several small companies if she wanted to. But knowing Rose, she funneled a great deal of her income into charities.

Sylvie froze. Of course. That was exactly what Rose had done. And one of those charities was named Sylvie Bennett. Her aching heart was momentarily warmed as she realized that her college scholarship had been no accident. Nor had her job offer from Colette before she'd even graduated. And the very affordable rent that allowed so many young women with decidedly modest incomes to live in the gracious old mansion on Amber Court had "subsidy" written all over it, she thought tenderly. What a wonderful woman Rose was, despite the heartbreak she'd surely suffered when her parents rejected her.

The meeting ended shortly before five o'clock. The moment Marcus concluded his speech, there was a general surge to the front of the room as enthusiastic employees worked their way forward to talk with either Marcus or Rose.

Sylvie turned to Meredith. "I'll see you at dinner."

Meredith narrowed her big blue eyes. "I heard you've resigned. I didn't believe it until now, but it's true, isn't it?"

Sylvie nodded wordlessly.

"Why? I thought you and Marcus—"

She stopped when Sylvie held up a restraining hand. "Don't. Please? Just—don't." And before her friend could say anything else, Sylvie slipped out of the room.

She went to Rose's apartment at six as they'd planned. When Rose opened the door, Sylvie moved close and embraced her, feeling a lump rise in her throat as the older woman's motherly arms closed around her. The warm atmosphere of Rose's homey apartment furnished in soft, soothing colors and gorgeous, gleaming pieces of antique furniture always gave her a sense of belonging.

"Thank you," Sylvie whispered. "For everything."

Rose patted her back. "Thank *you*, dear girl," she said. "One of my biggest regrets was that Mitch and I could never have a child of our own. Since you and I found each other, I've realized that biology plays a very small part in loving a child. Watching you blossom has been one of the greatest joys of my life.''

Sylvie tried to speak, stopped and put a hand to her mouth. She was very afraid she was going to break down and sob like a child. Finally, Rose put a warm arm around her and turned her toward the dining room. ''Let's join the others. We'll have plenty of time to talk later.''

Lila, Jayne and Meredith were there already, and the room fell silent as Sylvie and Rose walked in.

''Let me guess,'' Sylvie said, striving for a light tone. ''You weren't discussing the weather.''

Lila's cheeks turned pink and Meredith looked chagrinned. But Jayne grinned at her. ''We were sharing the dirt we have on you. Since you haven't talked to a single soul, we're reduced to exchanging rumors.''

The blunt words relieved the tense atmosphere as nothing else could have and they all laughed.

''I promise to explain everything,'' Sylvie said. Then she turned to Rose, who had taken a seat beside her on a loveseat. ''But right now, I'm dying to know the real story about Rose *Colette* Carson.''

''I'll second that.'' Meredith held up a wineglass in a mock toast.

Sylvie relaxed mentally. The last thing she wanted to do was rehash the events that had led to her taking the job in California. She couldn't work up any enthusiasm for the new position and she was very afraid it would show. With any luck, she could escape without getting into all of that tonight.

Over dinner, they admired Rose's Christmas tree, decorated with glistening antique fruit ornaments. ''They've been in my family for generations,'' Rose told them. As they ate, she talked about her childhood. She'd grown up an only child immersed in her family's jewelry design business. "It was a given that someday the company would be mine, even though I was a, ah, a somewhat difficult child," Rose said, her gaze faraway in the past. "I didn't always appreciate the opportunity." Her gaze focused and the familiar twinkle appeared as she gently mocked herself. "But eventually I settled down and began to work from the bottom of the business up, as my father believed I should. Not long after I began working in the design department, I created a brooch made of amber and several precious metals—"

"*Our* brooch?" asked Lila incredulously.

Rose smiled. "The very same." Her smile faded. "My father didn't like it one little bit, said it was too different from Colette's standards. The head designer was a bit kinder. He told me my work was 'ahead of its time,' whatever that meant. I argued with my father and we got into a huge fight. I felt like I had when I was a rebellious little girl, disappointing my parents, never meeting their expectations. I stomped out of the office and started to walk home, but as I was leaving, I ran into a young man who'd recently been hired in sales for Colette." She smiled in a coy manner, a youthful expression that surprised Sylvie and made her realize anew what a beauty Rose must have been thirty years ago. "I literally ran into him in the doorway of the office. Knocked us both down, in fact."

Meredith leaned forward. "Was it love at first sight?"

Rose nodded, her dreamy expression leaving them in no doubt. "It was. His name was Mitch Carson. The first thing he did when he helped me to my feet was compliment me on the striking brooch I was wearing. I knew right away that any man who could see the value in my design was special. Besides," she added with a wicked grin, "he was the sexiest man I'd ever met. I wanted to throw myself into his arms and beg him to kiss me!"

Lila sighed. "That's so romantic."

Jayne snickered.

"I mean, it's romantic that he saw the beauty in her design," Lila said, sticking out her tongue at Jayne.

"He was a very romantic man." Rose looked down at the diamond rings she still wore. "But my parents didn't care for him. He encouraged me to experiment with my designs. He took me sailing and dancing and to the races, all activities of which my parents didn't approve."

"But why?" asked Sylvie, thinking of the precious moments she'd spent dancing in Marcus's arms. Those memories would have to last her a lifetime.

Rose shrugged. "I think they were afraid I might have too much fun," she said dryly. "My parents were quite straitlaced and old-fashioned."

"I can't believe it," Jayne said. "You're nothing like that."

"You can thank Mitch," Rose told her. "My parents threatened to disinherit me if I continued my relationship with him. I knew if I listened to them I'd wind up a conservative, judgmental old grump just like they each had become. So Mitch and I eloped. When my father found out, he threatened me again with disinheritance. So Mitch and I moved to California. I never heard from my father again, although my mother told me years later how he had regretted losing touch." She shook her head sadly. "He was too proud to admit he was wrong."

"So…what brought you back to Youngsville?" Meredith asked.

Rose gripped her fingers together and took a deep breath. "Mitch and I had nearly thirty wonderful years together. The only thing that would have made us happier would have been to have a child. But it never happened. And then he was killed in a sailing accident before his fiftieth birthday.''

There was a heavy silence in the room. Sylvie slid her chair closer and put an arm protectively around Rose. ''We're so sorry,'' she whispered.

Rose looked at her, her eyes shiny with tears. ''I'm not,'' she said. Then she repeated, ''I'm not. Mitch and I loved each other so much. I wouldn't have changed one day of our lives together. He was a vital, vibrant person who met each new day at top speed, and I wouldn't have changed him even if I'd known how it was going to end.''

Lila was crying, and Jayne grabbed a travel pack of tissues from her purse and passed them over. ''So you came home after you were widowed?''

''Not right away. I stayed in California for another few years, but after my father had a fatal heart attack my mother begged me to come home and take over Colette. She was just a simple soul who'd been happy to be a housewife all her life. My father dominated her thinking, and she didn't know a thing about the business. I couldn't refuse her, although I did refuse to get involved. I simply held the family stock and voted.''

''And bought this place and named it for your beautiful brooch,'' Sylvie added.

''That's exactly right.'' Rose patted her knee affectionately.

''So how did Marcus talk you into becoming involved with Colette again?'' Jayne asked. Sylvie tried not to flinch at the sound of his name. She caught Meredith's sidelong glance but she didn't acknowledge it.

''One of the things that led to my estrangement with my father was his obsession with exclusivity,'' Rose told her. "When Marcus spoke to me about making Colette's jewelry more affordable, the idea held more appeal than he could have known. Besides," she said, smiling broadly, "that man does not take no for an answer."

There was an awkward silence as her words rang through the room.

"Now," said Rose hastily, "I have Christmas presents for you girls."

"But Rose," Sylvie protested, "I didn't bring mine down."

"Me, either," Meredith said.

"That's all right." Rose stood and walked to a gorgeous antique sideboard against one wall. "This is a special sort of thing. I didn't want to wait." She turned and came back to the four seated women, distributing a large legal-size envelope entwined with silver and red ribbons to each of them.

"What are these?" Lila asked, clearly mystified.

"I'm not shy," Sylvie declared. "I'll open mine." The others followed suit and in a moment, they were reading the papers they'd withdrawn from the envelopes. There was a hushed silence that grew steadily more electric as they began to realize what they held.

"Rose!" Sylvie leaped to her feet. "You can't do this!"

"Of course I can," Rose said comfortably, smiling at her shock. "What use do I have for Colette stock now? I'm giving each of you a twelve percent share in the company."

"But Rose," Jayne protested, "this is your heritage. We can't accept this."

"And it's your income, too," Lila added, ever practical.

Rose only smiled. "I've made more than enough in

dividends over the years to keep me for the rest of my
life. As for my heritage…'' She looked around, catching
the eyes of each of the women seated in her home. ''I
am the last living Colette. I've seen how much each of
you cares about this company, and how hard you've all
worked to try to save it.'' She swallowed. ''Each of you
has become special to me. You're like the daughters I
would have loved to have had. And I hope you'll accept
this gift in the spirit of love with which I give it.''

''Of course we will.'' Meredith's soft heart couldn't
bear to see anyone in distress. As one, they all got to
their feet and went to Rose. And as they shared a warm,
tearful group embrace, Sylvie wondered how on earth she
could leave Youngsville and all the people she loved so
much.

Two hours later, Sylvie quietly let herself back into
her dark apartment. She switched on the small lamp on
the table in her entry hall and hung up her coat, then
turned—

And gasped as she pressed a hand to her heart in shock.
Marcus sat in the white recliner in her living room. ''How
did you get in here?'' she demanded. ''You scared me
silly!''

''Rose gave me her key,'' he said. He didn't rise, simply watched her from the shadows.

Rose gave him a key? Why would Rose—?

''I guess she thought we had things to discuss,'' he
said, as if he knew what she was thinking.

Her heart was pounding so hard she was afraid he
could hear it. Her hands shook as she laid Rose's gift on
the table and clasped them in front of her. ''Rose was
wrong,'' she said quietly. ''We have nothing to talk
about. You did a lovely thing today and I thank you for

it, as I'm sure many of the others at that meeting did already. But—"

"Why?" he interrupted.

She looked at him blankly, still stunned by his presence. "Why what?"

"Why did I do it?" He rose and came toward her with slow, deliberate steps. "Why did I decide to keep Colette, and even to expand the company?"

"I don't know," she said, stifling irritation. "Why do you do anything? I'm certainly not the one to ask."

"What if I said you were?" he said softly.

Sylvie grabbed on to her patience with both hands, feeling herself perilously near tears. Why couldn't the man just go away and let her suffer in peace? "I'm afraid I'm not up for a circuitous conversation like you seem to have in mind." She spread her hands. "Look, Marcus, I don't know why you're here. Can't we *please* let this thing between us die with good grace? I don't do on-again off-again very well and—"

"I'm not the one who 'turned off' this last time," he said, and for the first time she heard a weary note of something that sounded almost like pain in his voice. "And I want to know why you did. Why did you decide to take a job in California?"

"It was a good offer. I couldn't really refuse."

"I'll make you a better one."

It was the final straw. "I don't want an offer from you!" she cried, her voice breaking. "I don't want anything from you! Now get out and leave me alone."

"Not a chance." He grabbed her elbows and hauled her into his arms, trapping her hands between them before she could take a swing at him like she was about to do. "You're stuck with me for the next fifty years or so."

* * *

Sylvie collapsed against his chest, crying wildly as if her heart were broken.

Marcus felt his own heart contract painfully. He'd never meant to cause her pain. Never meant to hurt her so badly. His Sylvie was a fearless, feisty soul, and for her to break down so completely was proof of how close to the bone the hurt went.

As carefully as if she were made of glass, he gathered her into his arms and carried her to the couch, sinking down with her in his lap and rocking her as if she were a child. "Sweetheart," he said, "please don't cry. Tell me how I hurt you so I can fix it." He knew he sounded desperate, but he didn't care because he *was*. "The past few days," he told her bent head as he caressed her back, "the past few days have been hell. Thinking about you on the other side of the damn country is making me crazy. What made you decide to do this?"

"I heard you," she said in an accusatory tone muffled in his sweater. "I don't know why you changed your plans, but I *heard* you telling someone to get started on the Colette...paperwork..." Her voice trailed away and he almost saw the lightbulb coming on.

"And that's why you threw me out of your life?" he asked incredulously. "Because you overheard a snippet of a conversation and drew your own conclusions?" Abruptly he was so mad he wanted to shake her, and he took her arms and set her aside as he sprang to his feet.

But she had rallied. She bounced to her feet as well, and the light of battle with which he was more familiar was in her eye. "No," she threw back at him, "that's *not* why. Although I admit I did misunderstand what I heard. Which is what started this whole thing. But I'm not sorry, Marcus. You know why? Because me taking that job in San Diego just speeds up the inevitable.''

"What inevitable?'' he roared.

"The *inevitable end* of this relationship,'' she shouted. "The end of me loving a man who can't love me back. I'm going to San Diego and you know what? When I get there, I'm going to start looking for someone to love. And I'll find him. And then—'' Her breath was starting to hitch and she was having trouble getting the words out. "And then—I'll—forget you. I swear—I will.'' She was crying again and he couldn't stand it.

"No, you won't,'' he said with more confidence than he felt. "You'll never forget me.'' He grabbed her and held her tightly against him, looking into her beautiful brown eyes as he spoke. "Because I'll follow you. You want the words? Fine. I love you. *I love you*, Sylvie,'' he repeated, "and if you think I'm letting you go anywhere you can damn well think again. You're staying right here in Indiana and you're marrying me. Got it?''

"I'm…marrying you?''

"You're marrying me.'' He pushed her into the nearest chair and lowered himself to one knee, taking her hands in his. "I do love you, Sylvie, and I need you so much it scares me. I guess I was afraid to admit it to myself because I knew how much power that would give you. Now will you say you'll marry me?''

But she didn't light up with happiness. Instead, she pulled her hands from his and laced her fingers together in her lap. "Loving someone doesn't mean giving them power over you,'' she told him. "It's choosing to share love and—and life decisions. I don't think you know how to do that, Marcus.''

"I'll learn," he said. "And you have things to learn, too."

She frowned. "Like what?"

"People who love each other work through their disagreements and miscommunications. They don't simply quit or run away when things are going poorly." He touched a finger to her lips when she would have cut in. "I realize you didn't have a role model to teach you about marriage when you were a kid. But you've seen Wil and Maeve. Do they ever fight?"

Sylvie rolled her eyes. "Do they ever!" Then she sobered. "But you didn't exactly have a great role model, either. What if we screw it up?"

"I want what your friends have," he told her. "My father let pride ruin his marriage and his whole life. I promise you that will never happen to me. To us." He dared to take her hand again. "I have something to give you." He smiled. "It's even more appropriate after this conversation."

He reached sideways, retrieving the envelope he'd laid on the coffee table earlier. "Consider this your first wedding gift," he said, handing her the envelope.

Her gaze flashed warily to his, then to the envelope. Slowly, she accepted it and withdrew the document inside. As she read it, her eyes grew wide. "But this is half of your Colette stock! You can't do this."

"Yes, I can," he said, smiling at her stunned face. "Now you and I each hold twenty-six percent. Which means we have to work together with Rose to make the right decisions for our company."

She tried to hand the paper back to him. "No, that's not true. Rose just gave me twelve percent of her stock as a Christmas gift. She also gave away the rest. This—"

she indicated the envelope, "would make me the majority stockholder! You'd better think about this."

He started to laugh. He couldn't help it, as he thought of how much trouble those blasted shares of Colette stock had caused between Sylvie and him. "You'll be able to oust me if you want to," he said. Then he got himself under control. "But instead, I hope you'll marry me. I want to be at your side for the rest of our lives."

Sylvie started to tear up again. "Rose said you weren't a man to take no for an answer," she told him. "So I guess I'd better say yes."

Elation flooded his system. "It's about time!" He reached into his pocket and retrieved the small velvet box with the Colette logo on it. "Here's your second gift. I want to get it on your finger before you get mad at me again."

"I might get mad at you," she said soberly, "but I promise I will never run away again. We'll just have to work out our problems." When he flipped up the lid on the box, she gasped in shock. "It's from the Everlasting collection! I helped design this promotion."

"I thought it was appropriate, since the company did bring us together."

"This is so special," she said as he slipped it onto her ring finger. "I never expected to wear a Colette engagement ring!"

"I thought we might want to change the name of the company." He sketched a large sign in the air. "Grey & Colette."

She had tears in her eyes as she came into his arms.

He felt the sting of a few unmanly tears of his own. He'd come close to losing her. Too close. "I love you," he told her again.

"And I love you." Her response was instant, fervent as she pressed her soft curves against him and lifted her mouth for his kiss.

"There's just one problem," she whispered into his neck a few minutes later.

"What?" There was no problem they couldn't overcome together.

"It should be 'Colette & Grey.'"

Epilogue

Sylvie had never really allowed herself to dream of a wedding before she'd met Marcus. But once she'd begun to plan, she'd done it with a vengeance. She'd decided that June was the perfect month for marriage.

June in Indiana was a glorious month of temperate days and cool nights with low humidity. Late spring bulbs and early summer perennials waved in the breezes off the lake and the sky was nearly always a glorious clear blue.

Sylvie's wedding day was no exception. They'd taken a bit of a risk and planned the reception outdoors on the terrace of the country club, and the chance had paid off. Women in floating summer dresses and men who had long since discarded their jackets danced to the music of the same orchestra that had played on the night of Marcus and Sylvie's first date. Lila, Meredith and Jayne stood out among the crowd, all attired in the vivid sky-blue gowns Sylvie had chosen for her attendants. Each of them was dancing with the man she loved, each looking radiantly happy.

Looking around for her groom, Sylvie felt a rush of tender emotion swell her heart when she located him kneeling beside Maeve's wheelchair with one hand over the older woman's as they shared what appeared to be an uproarious joke. He glanced up at her, catching her eye in a private smile, and with a final word to Maeve, crossed the terrace to her side.

"Having fun?" he murmured in her ear as he drew her from the group of women with whom she'd been talking and fed her a tidbit from one of the passing waiters' trays of *canapés*.

"Yes," she said. "Loads of fun. Isn't this wonderful, seeing all of our friends here together?"

He nodded. "Especially since they're all here to witness the fact that I finally managed to make you Mrs. Marcus Grey."

"Sylvie Grey." She tested the sound of the name on her lips. "Sylvie Bennett-Grey. Grey-Bennett."

"Grey," Marcus said definitely. "Just Sylvie Grey. I'm a traditional guy."

"Kidding." She chuckled. "It's so easy to pull your leg."

He bared his teeth and tugged her into his arms, nuzzling her neck as she squealed and squirmed. "I can see you're going to require a strong hand."

"All right, you two." Rose's fond tones cut through their laughter. "It's time to cut the cake. You'll have to save the snuggling for later."

"With pleasure," Marcus murmured in her ear as they followed the woman who had given Sylvie away at the altar.

Sylvie shivered as a frisson of anticipation danced down her spine. After six months, their lovemaking was still as fresh and special as it had been that very first night. More so, now that she knew he loved her.

A small commotion near the cake table caught her eye as they neared and she forgot her private thoughts as she saw Nick helping Lila to a chair. Her face was white and she looked distinctly ill, but as Sylvie rushed over, Lila was sipping a glass of fruit juice under Nick's eagle eye.

"Are you all right?" Sylvie demanded.

Lila smiled, and when she glanced up at her dark-haired husband, they exchanged a look so nakedly intimate that Sylvie felt it was too private to be witnessed. "I'm fine," she assured the group that had assembled.

"You don't look fine," Jayne said baldly. "You look like you have the 'flu' or something."

Lila smiled again. "Or something." She took a deep breath. "I wasn't going to do this on your wedding day," she said apologetically to Sylvie, "but...what I have is a nine-month condition that—"

"Lila!" Rose's eyes filled with tears as she leaped forward to embrace the young woman. "You're expecting?"

Nick grinned from ear to ear. "She is. We are."

"When?" Rose demanded.

Lila put a hand over the older woman's. "You'll be getting your first adopted grandchild at Christmas," she told Rose. She looked around at the group. "So don't any of you even think about going out of town for the holidays!"

"This is a *wonderful* wedding gift," Sylvie told her friend. "I'm so glad you shared your news with us today."

After the cake was cut, the orchestra struck up the first

dance, and soon the floor was filled with celebrating guests. Sylvie took a break after the first half an hour, heading for the table where Lila was still resting. Jayne and Meredith soon joined them and they all spent a few moment quizzing Lila about her newly discovered pregnancy.

"Adam and I want to start a family soon, too," Meredith said dreamily. "I can't wait to hold our first child in my arms."

"I bet Christmas seems a million years away right now," Jayne said to Lila.

The blonde nodded. "I wish it were tomorrow!" Then she waved a hand at the dance floor. "So who's the handsome prince dancing with Rose?"

Sylvie and the others looked in the direction she pointed. Rose was wrapped in a surprisingly close embrace with a tall, distinguished-looking silver haired man on the dance floor.

"Why, that's Ken Vance!" Sylvie exclaimed. "He's the producer of the Ingalls Park Theatre."

"A friend of yours?" Jayne inquired.

"A friend of Marcus's," Sylvie replied absently. "A lovely man. In fact, he'd be perfect for Rose."

"They look pretty perfect to me right now," Jayne said, chuckling.

Rose and Ken were completely absorbed with one another. As the women watched, the pair snuggled even closer. Ken's jaw rested near Rose's temple, and each of them had their eyes closed as they drifted slowly in time to the music.

"Oh! She's wearing the brooch today, isn't she?" Meredith breathed.

"She wore it to all of our weddings," Lila affirmed.

"Well," Jayne announced, "that's the end of widowhood for Rose.'' She made a show of dusting off her hands and they all smiled.

Marcus chuckled as he and the other men joined their wives in time to hear the last of the conversation, pulling Sylvie into the warm circle of his arms. ''Do you honestly believe that little pin has anything to do with...'' His words trailed off as all the women pivoted to stare at him.

Nick grinned, indicating the couples ranged around him. ''You don't?''

Marcus opened his mouth. Then his gaze shifted to Rose and Ken, and he nodded his head slowly. ''I'm fast becoming a believer.''

* * * * *

Look for Anne Marie Winston's
BILLIONAIRE BACHELORS: RYAN,
coming next month
in Silhouette Desire.

January 2002
THE REDEMPTION OF JEFFERSON CADE
#1411 by BJ James

Don't miss the fifth book in BJ James' exciting miniseries featuring irresistible heroes from Belle Terre, South Carolina.

MEN of Belle Terre

February 2002
THE PLAYBOY SHEIKH
#1417 by Alexandra Sellers

Alexandra Sellers continues her sensual miniseries about powerful sheikhs and the women they're destined to love.

SONS OF THE DESERT

March 2002
BILLIONAIRE BACHELORS: STONE
#1423 by Anne Marie Winston

Bestselling author Anne Marie Winston's Billionaire Bachelors prove they're not immune to the power of love.

MAN OF THE MONTH

Some men are made for lovin'—and you're sure to love these three upcoming men of the month!

Available at your favorite retail outlet.

Where love comes alive™